In Love with the Slacker

AN ALASKA SUNRISE ROMANCE

MELISSA STORM

Editor: Megan Harris

Cover & Graphics Designer: TM Franklin

Proofreader: Falcon Storm

Partridge & Pear Press

To all the beautiful girls, especially the one I call "daughter"

About this Book

Taylor Hunt loves her Army life, but she hates being stationed in Anchorage. She's always longed for adventure, for a cause worth fighting for, to prove herself—and she isn't going to accomplish any of that so far away from the action. She's just biding her time until her transfer request comes through, and a certain local slacker wants to spend every moment with her while they wait. Add in a demanding cat and a curious moose, and away we go.

This quick, light-hearted romance from a New York Times bestselling author is sure to put a smile on your face and a song in your heart!

One

Noah Rockwell wanted to go home.

And by the time Lolly Winston had completed her second encore, he'd already mapped out his quickest path to the exit. If he rushed, he could be home and in bed while the others were still fighting their way out of the parking lot.

"Give Lolly my best," he shouted in his brother's ear as he clapped him on the shoulder.

Oscar turned toward Noah, taking his eyes off his new bride for the first time that evening. "You're leaving? Aren't you going to come backstage?"

"Not tonight. I gotta open the store tomorrow."

Oscar rolled his eyes and gave his brother a quick hug. "Go on, then. Get your beauty sleep."

Normally Noah would fight back. After all, Oscar was the mama's boy, not Noah, and certainly not their other brother, Sebastian, who was the most macho of them all. But right now, he just wanted to beat the rush.

Sure, he was happy for his little brother and all that. But when you worked in electronics for a living, the novelty of having a country music star in the family wore off fast. And as much as he loved Lolly, he didn't love all the excited teens that regularly stalked his store, hoping to get a peek of their favorite singer.

Annoying, that's what it was. Just like his stupid cat.

Sure enough, the moment Noah walked through his apartment door that night, his black and white tomcat, Billy Idol, hopped up on the counter and fixed him with an evil stare.

"What?" Noah moaned. "Why is everyone in my life so demanding lately? Especially you?"

Billy walked a few steps, then looked up at Noah with a mischievous glint in his feline eyes.

"Oh no, you don't!" Noah rushed across the apartment, but it was too late for the half-empty soda bottle.

With a quick nudge and a strategic bat from his

cat roommate, the bottle of Dr. Pepper fell onto the linoleum floor with a loud fizzing *pop!*

"Bad, *bad* cat!" Noah cried as sticky brown leaked across the floor. "Why did I ever agree to take you in the first place?" he growled, and the cat growled right back.

He knew exactly why he'd taken in the irritating animal, and he'd probably do it all over again, too. Sure, the cat bugged him to no end, but having it here made his mother happy—and he did love his mom, even though she was kind of annoying, too.

Noah and his brothers couldn't have predicted how attached their mother would become to her new cat friend and its litter of kittens. So attached, in fact, that rather than adopting out, their mom had made sure each of the kitties ended up with a family member. Even his cousin, Charlie, and her new husband, Will, hadn't been spared, despite already having two large dogs of their own.

Billy Idol paced back and forth on the counter as Noah sopped up the mess with a wad of paper towels. His fuzzy black feline mustache twitched in disapproval, even though he clearly liked watching Noah suffer.

That meant it was time to activate the silent

treatment torture—his cat's absolute least favorite thing.

After a quick shower, Noah headed to bed, making sure to lock Billy Idol out of the bedroom.

Immediately, Billy Idol began to meow angrily from the hall and claw at the shut door.

"Go away!" Noah called out, but his words only set the cat off more.

How could a cat have changed his life so much? Weren't they supposed to be easy pets? He knew his brother was happier after having met and married Lolly, starting their charity organization together, and now settling into domestic life. There was no denying that Oscar's smile had grown a mile wide these days.

But as for Noah?

Well, this stupid cat was already more responsibility than he wanted. He liked serving as the manager of the same local electronics store he'd worked in since high school. He liked spending his paychecks on the latest video game or tech toy. He liked that his life was every bit as much play as it was work—although the cat was definitely starting to tip that balance.

Oscar and their mother often asked when Noah, being the oldest, would "finally" settle down, and

Noah always answered with, "Whenever I meet a girl worth settling for." The truth was, though, Noah couldn't even begin to imagine a woman perfect enough to make him give up his simple, happy life.

Well, *happy...* provided he could actually get some sleep that night.

Of course, it was at this moment the cat began making its horrible, demonic sounds. Noah couldn't stand to listen to this the whole night, so he begrudgingly kicked the covers off and let the furry nuisance into his room. Billy Idol immediately began to purr and tucked himself against the small of Noah's back in the bed.

As long as Noah did exactly what the cat wanted when he wanted it, they didn't have any problems.

And how on earth could a girlfriend be any different?

Yup. No, thank you, Noah thought as he finally drifted off to sleep.

Taylor Hunt was so bored.

She'd joined the Army for adventure, not to hang around base all day, watching as her brothers in arms challenged each other to a *Call of Duty* gaming marathon.

"C'mon, T-Hunt. Grab a controller!" one of them called, scooting over to make room for her on the couch.

Taylor scoffed. "Don't you guys realize we fight actual bad guys? Why would you want to play make-believe?"

Chuck—who had recently been promoted above them and wanted to make sure no one forgot it, even for a second—laughed. "Bad guys, huh? In Alaska? Where are they hiding? Are they behind the couch? In the fridge? Maybe they're out in the snow?"

Laughter rose all around the hall.

"You know what I mean," Taylor muttered under her breath.

"We gotta keep our skills sharp somehow. Only thing to fight around here is penguins."

Taylor sighed. "That's the South Pole."

"What about a pole?" Chuck asked, making a lewd gesture.

More immature laughter shot through the room.

She crossed her arms over her chest, sorely wishing she was somewhere else as she explained, "Penguins don't live in Alaska. Honestly, if you guys ever left the barracks, you'd know that."

"So are you going to play or not?"

"Not," Taylor said, grabbing the small messenger bag she used as a purse. "See you losers later."

"Aww, you're no fun!" Chuck and the others called, but quickly lost themselves in the game, moving on to heckle each other instead of her.

As much as Taylor loved working as a Unit Supply Specialist in the armed forces, she couldn't deny that she didn't quite fit in. And that was basically the story of her entire life.

In school, she'd been too much of a tomboy to fit in with the other girls. Now, her fellow soldiers never let her forget that she was a girl, different—one of the guys, except not exactly. They seemed to think of her as a little sister, even though most of them were the same age. That at least meant no one had tried to date her, but it also subjected her to a lot of ribbing.

Meanwhile, she was going crazy up here. There were fewer people, fewer job duties, less of everything. It being summer, there wasn't even snow—and that had been the only part of being stationed up north she'd actually looked forward to.

So, of course, she'd wasted no time in requesting a transfer. She preferred to return to her hometown of Charleston, but anywhere had to be better than here.

Driving around town now, she caught sight of a street festival, but decided against peopling for the day. She needed to find something a bit more relaxing to entertain her, to give her a break from the guys.

Maybe she should have just stayed at the barracks and played their stupid game. Up ahead, the big-box electronics store stood tall and bright amongst the smaller businesses surrounding it.

Maybe she could find a game of her own. Anything had to be better than *Call of Duty*. Seriously, anything.

Before she could overthink it, she parked her car at the far end of the lot, enjoying the fresh, crisp air as she jogged toward the entrance. It didn't take much to find the video games section, and it took even less time to notice the nearby employee who kept his eyes glued firmly on her as she browsed their selection.

"Army or Air Force?" he asked, striding over to stand beside her.

Taylor kept her eyes on the game in her hands, pretending to be absorbed in the back-of-box description. "Army," she mumbled.

"It's how you stand, the way you carry yourself," the man explained, even though she hadn't asked.

She nodded and continued to study the game, even though she'd already decided she didn't want it.

"Don't get that one," he said. "It's way too over-hyped and not actually very good. Can I help you find something better? By the way, I'm Noah Rockwell, the manager here."

At last she looked up at him, admitting to herself that he wouldn't be going away anytime soon. As soon as she did, she was greeted with warm, caramel eyes and a broad grin. His dark hair was shaggy and the ends touched his shirt collar—way out of regulation—though the rest of him was well groomed and clean.

"What do you recommend, then?" she asked, refusing to return his smile.

He raised one curious eyebrow. "Not going to tell me your name?"

"I don't see how knowing my name affects your ability to help me find a good game."

"*Touché*. If I find a game you like, will you tell me, then?"

"Sure." She wasn't sure why it mattered, but whatever would get her out of here fastest was what she would do.

"Okay, then. Follow me." Noah led her to the

other end of the aisle and plucked a game from the back of the display. "Here you go."

She accepted the box from him and read the description on the back, and—darn it—it did sound fun. Yup, a good, old fashioned role-playing game with magic and wizards and a totally immersive storyline was exactly what she needed to pass the rest of the weekend.

"You're really beautiful, you know that?" Noah said, moving a couple inches closer.

Taylor laughed softly to herself. "Yeah, okay," she answered. People called Taylor a lot of things, but *beautiful* had very rarely been one of them. Taylor was strong, hard-working, smart, funny, but she was not beautiful. That word had never felt like her, and it didn't feel like her now.

She lifted the game up to make a small barrier between her and the weird guy trying to compliment her. "Thanks for your help. I'll get this one."

As she turned to leave, he quickly circled around her, coming to stand before her in the aisle. "What about our deal? I find a game you like, and you tell me your name?"

"Just because I'm buying it, doesn't mean I like it. I need to play it first, right?"

He laughed and shook his head. "So it's going to be like that?"

She shrugged. "I guess it is."

As she finished making her way toward the checkout line, Noah called after her, "Come back and tell me what you think of it once you've had a chance to play."

She smiled inwardly, doubting very much that she would ever see Noah Rockwell again.

Two

Of course, the mysterious girl gamer had left quite an impression on Noah.

"She's got these amazing dark eyes," he reported to a very uninterested Billy Idol that night. "And she only smiled for a second, but I swear it was the most beautiful thing ever."

The cat turned in a circle and padded the couch with his two front paws before lying back down.

"But the best part?" Noah continued, having to confess his new crush to someone, even if it was just his stupid cat.

The cat began to close his eyes, but Noah clapped to startle him back awake.

"Listen to me here," he demanded. "I always listen to you and your ridiculous meowing."

Billy Idol flicked his tail, but kept his attention on Noah.

"So you can be nice sometimes after all?" Noah gave the cat a quick scratch between his ears before continuing on. "Anyway, the best part of everything, is that she's a gamer, AKA, we share the same interests, AKA I'm not saying I want a girl sweeping in here and changing our bachelor lives, but if I did— oh, Billy Idol—it would definitely be her."

Of course, Noah assumed he'd never see the secretive beauty again. She'd made it a point not to disclose her name, not to engage him in conversation, not to reveal anything about herself. As much as Noah wanted to get to know her, she seemed equally committed to preventing that from happening.

So imagine his surprise when she returned to his store a few weekends later. He heard her before he saw her. She stood at the counter, talking with the guys who manned the cell phone counter. "Yes, I'm looking for someone, actually. Is Noah Rockwell in?"

"That depends who's asking," he said as he closed the distance between them.

"Hi," she said, turning toward him with a start. She gave a brief almost smile before continuing. "My name is Taylor Hunt, and I just beat *The Four Talismans* video game. It was fantastic."

"Cool name, Taylor Hunt. Thank you for finally telling me. And here I thought I'd never see you again," he admitted.

"I realize that, but now that I've finished *Talismans*, I kind of need something new to play during my downtime. And, well, I figured any guy who could recommend such a fantastic game couldn't be so bad, after all."

"Let's take that one thing at a time," Noah said, taking a chance and placing a hand at the small of her back as he led her back toward the gaming section of the store. "First, you need another game. I'm going to recommend the *Dragon Age* franchise. That way you can hit them back to back, one after the other."

"Awesome, thank you." She reached for her tightly held ponytail, flicked it back behind her shoulders, and gave him a full-on smile.

Neither said anything for a moment, mostly because her huge grin caught Noah totally off guard. This was not the woman he remembered meeting a few weeks back. This new version of Taylor was somehow even better.

"I..." he began, forgetting where it was he had planned on going.

"You?" she prompted with a slight laugh.

"Yes, you," he redirected his line of thinking, at last remembering what he'd wanted to say. "*You* said you wanted to go out with me."

"I never said that."

"Then what was that whole 'any guy who could recommend such a great game can't be so bad?'"

"Me being nice?" She tried to hide her smile by looking away, but he caught it anyway.

"And what was coming in to ask for me by name? Which you remembered, by the way, almost a whole month later?"

"I..."

"Yes, you. *You* want to go out with me, so don't be shy."

She grunted and crossed her arms over her chest, but he saw right through her faked defenses. "I do not want to go out with you."

"Uh-huh, likely story."

"No, really. I'm not really on the market right now."

"Not on the market? Does that mean you have a boyfriend?"

She sighed now and looked back at the game display. "More like I'm out of stock."

"What does *that* mean?"

"It means..." She stopped to take a deep breath in. "It means I don't have a boyfriend, but also that I don't want one."

"Mixed signals much, Soldier?"

"Stop that. I just came in to get a new game."

"And?"

"And to ask if maybe you want to come over and play it with me sometime?"

"Yup, there it is."

"As friends, of course." She smiled again, this time trying to hide it behind her hand.

"Sure, friends."

"Stop twisting my words. Unless you want me to take back my invite."

"Okay, fine, you win. Now give me your number before you change your mind again."

They quickly exchanged numbers, then Noah asked, "So when are we getting together?"

"I don't know. I'll text you."

"Great. It's a date!"

"It's... You know what?" She groaned again and rolled her eyes, quickly turning on her heel then murmuring, "It's time for me to go, I think."

"Text me!" Noah called after her.

The fact that Taylor walked away laughing was a very good sign, indeed.

S ure, Taylor only wanted to be friends with Noah, but that didn't stop her palms from sweating and her breath from hitching as she tried to work up the courage to text him.

What are you doing tonight? She typed, hoping it sounded casual enough.

The response came almost immediately. *Hanging out with you ;)*

What did that winky face mean? Taylor shook her head, trying not to read too much into it and, instead, just focused on typing her next message. *Send me your address and I'll be over in a bit.*

As she watched the three shifting dots that meant Noah was typing a response, she decided to add: *Remember, it's not a date.*

The typing stopped for a few seconds and then started again. First came a message with Noah's home address, and then quickly after: *We'll see about that.*

Taylor shook her head. Wet hair clung to her collarbone as she did. This guy was certainly determined to change her mind. And she kind of liked that, despite herself.

Taking a deep breath, she stepped in front of the bathroom mirror. Should she let her hair air dry like usual or try to style it somehow? Wear it up or down? And for that matter, what did a girl wear when headed to a cute guy's apartment to play video games?

Oops.

Okay, so now she was admitting to herself that she liked this guy. It still didn't mean she wanted to date him. She didn't want to date anyone, especially considering she expected her transfer to come through any day. And also because her career was too important to get sidelined by a guy. Because it was never *just* a guy. Oh, it started with one "just a guy," but then there was marriage, babies in a baby carriage, and, just like that, her whole life would pass her by.

Nope. No, thank you.

Well, that settled that, but it still didn't help her figure out what she should wear.

She studied her face in the mirror, noticing that her cheeks were unnaturally red today, and deep bags puffed at the underside of her eyes. If she had some makeup, maybe she would have put it on to even out her complexion, but Taylor had never been a makeup girl. A quick coat of chapstick and a high and tight ponytail had always been enough—and it would be enough today, too.

Noah would just have to deal with it. After all, it's not like anyone expected guys to wear makeup. So why should they expect her to?

She was different enough already. In middle school, she'd stood a head taller than most of her classmates, boys and girls included. Heck, even her name was a boy's name. Nobody pictured a 5'11, raven-haired woman when they heard the name Taylor Hunt—and frankly, she couldn't blame them.

Of course, she felt comfortable with herself *now*, but her school days had been very different. The mean girls picked on her, and she often got called to the principal's office for fighting, even though it was just to defend herself.

In fact, she got so used to fighting that by the time she graduated, she decided she'd like to keep doing it in her adult life, too. Only this time she'd be fighting for something worthy—for her country, for the right for people like her to be free, to be themselves, and to not have to answer to anybody about it.

Except her experience with the Army had thus far involved zero fighting, unless you counted arguing with her bunkmates over who would choose the next movie.

No, the higher-ups continued to station her at remote bases, calling on her skills as a Unit Supply Specialist, saying she was needed here, was too valuable to send abroad.

Yeah, right.

A part of her died every time someone else got shipped off to Afghanistan or Iraq, leaving her behind to man the fort on home soil.

It was so... boring.

Such a waste.

At least for tonight, though, she had an adventure ahead of her. She liked that Noah was intent on pursuing her. It was fun to rebuff his advances, and frankly, it was fun just to banter and flirt for a change.

But she definitely could not get backed into a relationship. Because if she did, any chance of ever seeing adventure would disappear forever.

Three

Noah definitely hadn't expected Taylor to reach out to him, but he loved that she did. Unfortunately, the last-minute nature of their plans left him with barely any time to clean up. He'd only just managed to scoop Billy Idol's litter box and run the waste down to the dumpsters when Taylor pulled up in her sleek, shiny sedan.

"I thought you drove Humvees in the Army?" he joked as she ambled out of the car.

Taylor rolled her eyes and made a face. "Stereotype much?"

"Not at all. Just trying to get you figured out."

"Maybe there's nothing to figure out. Maybe I'm exactly what you see."

"Hmm, well, I do like what I see," he said, giving her a quick glance up and down. Her wet hair clung to the sides of her neck, and her oversized sweatshirt screamed "Not a date!" It screamed so loud that Noah knew Taylor was trying to convince herself just as much as she was him.

She cleared her throat and looked away, but not before he caught the rising blush on her cheeks. "Anyway, the car's a lease. Supposed to get good gas mileage, so seemed like a good choice to me."

"So you're an environmentalist? Interesting."

"I wouldn't go that far, but I will go away if you don't stop assessing me like I'm some kind of research project. Are we going to play this game or not?"

"Oh, we're going to play," he answered with a chuckle. "And I'm going to win."

"Never underestimate an opponent," she shot back, rising to her full height in a show of bluster. "Especially when that opponent is me."

Noah stared at her, unable to decide if she was being serious or trying to flirt. Either way, he'd find out soon enough.

"After you." He opened the door to the apartment building and stepped back to let her enter ahead of him.

They jogged up the stairs and returned to a very ornery kitty. Billy Idol let out a slow, irritated meow, drawing both of their attention to where he stood on the TV stand.

"I wouldn't have taken you as a cat person," Taylor said, side-eyeing him before striding over to say hello to Billy Idol.

"I'm not," Noah answered as the cat arched his back and hissed, then ran off to hide in the bedroom. "I'm a family person, and I couldn't say no when my mom asked me to take Billy Idol in."

"And you're an '80s pop music person, too? Seems *you're* the one who is full of surprises here." This time, she didn't even try to hide the smile as it bloomed upon her face.

"Again, that's all my mom. She was in a girl band in the '80s, my dad was in a hair metal band, and neither of them is willing to admit their favorite decade has ended."

"They sound like quite the pair." Taylor laughed as she sunk down onto the far end of his couch. "So if both of your parents are singers, does that mean...?"

He shook his head so hard, it was almost as if he *was* channeling his dad's hair metal days. "Heck no. I can't carry a tune to save my life."

"Prove it. Sing something for me."

He crossed his arms and scoffed. "No."

"Please?"

"Nope."

"What if we made a bet?"

He raised an eyebrow at her. "What did you have in mind?"

"Well, we're here to play some games. Let's play a few. If I win two out of three, you have to sing any song I pick."

"And if I win?"

"You won't," she answered with a completely straight face.

He laughed again, loving her competitiveness. "If I win..." He sunk onto the couch beside her, so their legs were touching, then turned toward her so their faces were hardly more than a few inches apart. He licked his lips and continued, "If I win, you have to kiss me."

A moment passed where she said nothing, but he caught the shiver that ran through her body. He also noticed the way her breath hitched and she blushed yet again. She could deny it all she wanted, but she clearly liked him, too.

And she wanted that kiss, too.

"Since I won't be losing," she said, her swagger

having returned after the brief lapse. "You've got yourself a deal."

&

Taylor groaned as the "kill cam" showed how Noah had butchered her character in the game for what felt like the millionth time. "I hate first person shooters."

"C'mon, fair's fair. You chose the first game, so it was my turn to pick."

"Yeah, but you knew I didn't want to do this one."

"I didn't know you would be so bad at it though."

Taylor threw her controller at Noah, and he fell back on the couch laughing. Even though she was losing—and badly—she was still having a great time.

"You totally knew it. That's why you picked this one!"

"Fine, fine. Put in something new, and I'll go grab us some snacks from the kitchen."

Taylor sifted through his collection of video games, which had to be the largest she'd ever seen from anyone. Was this Noah's entire life—flirting with strangers, fighting with a cat, and playing video games? It didn't seem bad, actually—just the complete opposite of her world of discipline, order, and often boredom.

"How about some taquitos and hummus?" Noah called from the kitchen, just as Taylor had settled on one of her old favorites, a game she hoped and prayed she could beat him at to help even the score a bit better.

"That's a really weird combination," she said, pulling up her selected game on the screen.

"Well, you don't have to eat them together. I just don't have a lot in my fridge right now... *or ever,*" he muttered that last part under his breath, but Taylor still managed to hear it.

She laughed, feeling more relaxed that she was at least partially in control. "You're such a typical meat-head guy."

"I don't know whether to take offense to that or feel honored," he called, poking his head out from the kitchen for a second.

"Tell me something different about you, something unique."

"Nope," he shouted as he moved out of her line of sight once more. "I've been an open book this whole time. I think it's time you revealed your dark secrets."

Taylor laughed, this time from shock. "Dark secrets, huh? Well, I haven't got any. What you see is what you get."

Noah came back into the living room then and dropped a couple plates of food onto the coffee table. Looking her up and down, he broke out into a smile and said, "Well, what I see is a gorgeous woman who doesn't realize how gorgeous she is and despite being so very, very gorgeous, she can still bro out and have a good time."

"Did you say *gorgeous* enough?" she asked, embarrassed.

"One more time? Because really, you are *gorgeous.*" He nodded as if doing so would get her to agree. Hardly.

She tore his eyes away from him and studied a stain on the carpet across the room. "Umm, thanks, but that's not what I meant," she mumbled. "I'm just an ordinary tomboy who likes rules and order but is also willing to throw down in a fight."

When she raised her eyes to look at him again, Noah was wearing a huge, mischievous grin, his mind having clearly gone other places. "Not what I meant at all!"

"Why do you turn bright red when I tell you how pretty you are?"

"Because we're friends and *only* friends," she said aloud, then added in her mind, *And I don't believe you when you say that.*

"Yes, I know. We've been over all that, but we also made a friendly bet. And you lost." He leaned in close to her again and wiggled his eyebrows.

She couldn't help but laugh. Half of her actually did want him to collect on their bet, but she also knew how much she had to lose by getting involved with Noah or with anyone. She'd always known that dating a fellow soldier would create a world of trouble for her, so she'd pushed down the desire—deeper, deeper, until she could no longer find it.

Sure, Noah wasn't a soldier, but he was still a man and his life was here in Anchorage, while hers was with the Army and where ever they decided to send her next.

Oh, why was she playing with fire like this? Was she truly that bored back at base that she needed to stir up some trouble to feel alive again?

Noah backed away again and handed her a controller. "Even though I've clearly won and there's no way you can recover, I would never make you do something that made you feel uncomfortable."

She swallowed the huge lump that had formed in

her throat, finally feeling as if she could breathe freely again. "Thank you, I appreciate that."

"I will, however, remind you at every opportunity that you lost a bet and owe me a kiss."

"Then it looks like I'll be keeping my distance."

"We both know that's not true. You'll be back, and I'll have my kiss before the end of the week." He leaned in close again and gave her a smoldering gaze.

"Back away, lover boy. If you try anything funny, I'll break both of your arms."

"I don't doubt you would." Noah laughed. "Now show me what you got."

The intro music of their new game swelled, and the return to their competition allowed Taylor to relax and enjoy herself for the rest of the night.

No arm-breaking required.

Four

Noah slept in late the next morning. After all, it was his one day off that week, and he planned on moving as little as possible.

Those plans flew out the window, however, when his brother, Sebastian, banged through the front door and into the apartment. "Big brother, wake up!" he called, kicking at Noah's bedroom door.

Billy Idol growled and ran to hide under the bed, scratching Noah with his hind claws as he did. Why had he ever agreed to give Sebastian a key to his place?

"Go away," he grumbled, pulling the pillow over his head with a groan.

"I hope you're dressed, because I'm coming in!" Sebastian said right before he barged in and hopped down onto Noah's bed, crushing him in the process.

"I'm sleeping here!" Noah moaned from beneath the pillow.

"Not anymore," Sebastian insisted.

"Why are you so annoying? Why are you *here?*"

"Aww, you love me and you know it."

Noah pried the pillow from his head and shoved it at Sebastian's smug face. "Right now you are my least favorite person on the planet," he said truthfully.

"I brought you donuts, though." Sebastian pushed the pillow aside, then shoved a box at him. The inviting smell of greasy goodness eased Noah's annoyance some.

"Get off me," he said, pushing his brother to the floor. "And give me a chocolate glazed."

"Here you go." Sebastian handed a donut over with flair and a huge, goofy grin.

"Now what do you want?"

"What makes you think I want anything other than the company of my favorite big brother?"

Noah glared at him, but Sebastian just shrugged.

"Okay, okay, fine," Sebastian said after a few

blessed moments of silence passed between them. "Maybe there is a small, tiny, itty-bitty something."

Noah smirked at how well he knew his baby brother. "There it is."

"I know it's your weekend with the plane and everything, but I thought maybe you wouldn't mind switching it out for one of mine. The caribou hunt is starting up and I got pulled in the lottery this year, and I don't have to work, so..." He flopped back down onto the end of the bed and clasped his hands together in an overdramatic prayer. "Please, Noah. Please!"

Noah picked at his donut, eating it slowly just to torture his brother as payback for waking him up early on the weekend. He'd actually completely forgotten that it was his turn to take their dad's small hunting plane out this weekend, but now that Sebastian had reminded him, he had the perfect idea.

"Sorry, bro. I'm going out this weekend. You'll have to wait your turn."

"But you don't even have a caribou license this year! Where are you planning to go?"

"Fishing," Noah answered confidently, reaching for a second donut from the box.

Sebastian was too quick, though. He'd already flung himself off the bed and over to the nightstand, grabbing the box away before Noah could help himself to a second glob of heavenly fried dough.

"Fishing can wait, and you know that. Why are you being such a pill about this?"

"I'm just looking forward to it is all. We have the schedule for a reason, you know."

"Fine, then let me come with you. Drop me off and you can fish to your heart's content. We don't even have to talk to each other. But, you will have to pick me up after a few days."

"No can do."

"I'll pay for fuel! C'mon, you know that plane seats two. Stop being such a jerk."

"Yup, it seats two. And with that big head of yours, I think you count as one and a half."

Sebastian quirked an eyebrow at him and sighed. "So what's really up? Who *is* going with you? Oscar? Dad?"

"Nope, somebody else."

"Who?"

"You don't know her."

"Her? What? No, no, no, Noah. You aren't going soft like Oscar, are you? You know if you get yourself married, then Mom will never leave me alone. Don't do it, Noah. Think of your baby brother."

"Don't do what? Go fishing? Stop being ridiculous."

"I kind of hate you right now, you know?"

"Fine by me. You can go now, but leave the donuts."

"Seriously? You're blowing me off for some girl, and you won't even tell me about her?"

"That is correct. Bye bye now." He walked his brother to the door and shut him out.

"You suck. You know that, don't you?" Sebastian called through the door before finally trudging away.

Noah watched his brother make his way across the parking lot below and waited to be sure he wouldn't be coming back before texting Taylor. He decided to start the exchange with: *Good morning :)*

She was already up and answered him right away. *Hi. Still don't want to date you.*

All I said was good morning.

Yeah with a smiley face! I know what that :) means...

Jeez. Jump to conclusions much?

Okay, then why are you texting me?

To ask you out

!!!

Not on a date

???

To go fishing

Are you serious right now?

Yup, fishing is definitely not a date. It's got blood, guts, and gore. All the good stuff.

Where is there to fish around here?

I'll pretend like you just didn't ask that.

What? It's a legitimate question!

It's Alaska, there's water everywhere and more fish than people up here. I'm going to take you to one of my favorite spots.

So we can catch fish?

That's right.

And it's not a date?

Not unless you want it to be...

The blood, guts, and gore thing sounds way more fun to me.

And that's why I like you so much. Does this mean you'll come?

Send me the details, and I'll see what I can do.

Taylor had to check and recheck the address Noah sent just to be sure she was in the right place. She'd expected to pull up to nature preserve, not a small airplane hangar. What kind of deluxe fishing trip was this?

She must have taken a wrong turn somewhere, and now she was late.

Really, really late.

As she pulled around the parking lot, preparing

to head back to the main road, she at last caught sight of Noah waving as he jogged toward her car.

"I was beginning to think you'd stood me up!" he puffed.

"And I'm beginning to think you've gotten me here under false pretenses," she said with a smirk, closing the door behind her.

He shot her a confused look. "Haven't you ever fished before?"

"Yeah, but it didn't require a plane."

"Then you've never done it right," Noah answered confidently. "Until now."

Taylor searched his face for any signs that he may be lying, but Noah stared back at her with an earnest expression and a contented smile.

"You said you have the whole weekend free, right?"

"Yes...?" She hesitated, still unsure of his intentions... or hers. Could she really spend all this time with him and keep her no dating rule in effect?

"Great, because we're going to need it. I've packed you an overnight bag with some basic essentials. Otherwise, we're roughing it."

No, this would be too hard. It wasn't a good idea. "I signed up for fishing, not to fly off to some unknown place and share a bed with you overnight!" she argued.

"Bed? Oh, no." He chuckled and shook his head. "Relax, we each have our own tent, and I promise to be a perfect gentleman. This is how Rockwell's fish. And since you're fishing with a Rockwell, you may as well do it right."

"You promise nothing funny is going on here?"

"*Fishy* maybe, but not funny. I promise."

"Good, because if you try anything, I'll brea—"

"Break both of my arms? So I've heard. Now are you in?"

They were just friends. She trusted him when he said that. She still didn't know if she could trust herself, but at least this weekend would be a great exercise in self-control. Taylor sighed and said, "Lead the way."

Noah did just that, bringing her to a small bush plane that hardly looked bigger than her car.

"And you're going to fly this?" she asked skeptically.

"As long as that's okay with you, ma'am?"

Oh, yeah, that definitely doused any sparks flying between them. "Ma'am? What am I, your mother?"

"Well, I just don't want you thinking this is a date or something," he countered with a wink.

"I don't know..." She wrung her hands together, searching for any excuse other than the fact that she was terrified of the tiny little air vehicle and its civilian pilot. "You didn't steal it, did you? I mean, who has their own plane? Are you some kind of secret prince or something?"

"A prince, really? Remember how I led with blood and guts here? And I'm not a thief, either. It's my Dad's plane, and I've been flying it since I was like fifteen. I swear it's safe, and besides, we don't really have that far to go."

"So maybe we should just drive."

"I think Ms. Tough Guy is scared. I also think she doesn't need to be."

"And *I* think you don't need to talk about me in third person like that. Okay, fine." She took a deep breath and hopped up onto the large pontoons before she could change her mind. "Let's do it."

As soon as she managed to sit down in the cramped cockpit, Noah handed her a rough-looking headset with big green ear muffs. "You're going to need these. It's pretty loud once we get going."

She nodded as she struggled to figure out the seatbelt.

Without hesitation, he reached across her and pulled a third strap from next to her that hosted another part of the intricate buckle. The droning of the plane drowned out whatever Noah had said, but he gestured to the headset again.

With shaking hands, Taylor adjusted the device over her ears like an old-timey telephone operator.

A tinny voice came across the speakers. "There you are. Sorry if it's a bit snug in here. Oh, and make sure you don't touch this knob here," he said, tapping a bright red dial.

She gulped down the bubbling fear rapidly rising in her diaphragm. "Okay. Where are the parachutes?"

Noah's laughter sounded as if it was coming from an empty can. "Why? You planning on jumping out of a perfectly good airplane?"

"No, I just want to make sure I'm being safe."

"Okay, in the interest of safety, I need you to look out that window and tell me if there are any planes or cars coming this way."

"Haha. Very funny."

"Okay, well, hope we don't hit anyone then," he said as the plane lurched forward.

"Wait!" she screamed into the headset. "Don't you need to call 'the tower' or something?"

Noah grinned. "You know, you're right. *Tower!"* He yelled as he gunned the plane forward, pushing

Taylor back into her seat as the noise of the engine ratcheted up. She could feel vibrations pulsing through the plane. She squeezed her eyes shut as she felt her chest beginning to compress.

"You can open them now," Noah's strong, confident voice said into the darkness.

"What?" she said, cracking one eye open.

"I said you can open your eyes. And maybe sit back a bit. You were pushing against the yoke during takeoff." He gestured to the oddly shaped steering wheel in front of her.

She muttered an apology, thoroughly embarrassed now.

"You don't have to be so tough all the time, you know. It's okay to admit you're scared. Or, I don't know... that you're beautiful."

"Okay, fine, I'm scared. Please don't do any crazy loop-de-loops or anything, okay? Let's just get there in one piece."

"See, was that so hard? How about the second part?"

"What more do you want from me? I already told you that your flying scares me. Maybe you should take a little less pride in that."

"Tell me that you're beautiful."

"Why would I say that about myself? People

don't say that about themselves, Noah. It makes them conceited."

"They should when they're as beautiful as you. Besides, I think if you say it, maybe you'll start to believe it, too."

"You are exhausting, you know that?" Taylor let some of the tension out of her tightly held muscles, finally beginning to relax even though they were still nowhere near the nice, safe ground.

"Oh, of course, I do. Now are you going to say it or what?"

She managed a smile, and from the bliss that lit up Noah's face, he'd caught it. "I'll tell you what is really beautiful," she said. "This scenery. Now shut up and let's enjoy it for a second."

He continued to wear a self-satisfied smirk on his handsome face, but thankfully dropped the topic.

"Look to the right, and you'll see a few mountain goats out for a graze," Noah said after a while.

Taylor turned in the direction he described and saw a line of fuzzy white blurs moving against the rocky mountains. Little specks of green, purple, and yellow dotted the blur below, and she imagined that the plant life must be every bit as beautiful as the expansive sky holding their plane like a safety blanket.

Noah continued to play tour guide as they flew, and soon she was so busy glancing from one beautiful thing to the next that she almost forgot to be afraid.

That is... until she spied the most beautiful thing of all.

And it wasn't the goats or the mountains or the rushing rivers... No, it was the man seated beside her who had truly captured her awe.

Five

N oah began the descent as gently as he could.

Still, Taylor squeezed her eyes shut tight and clutched onto his arm with one hand and her seat with the other. The lake loomed larger and larger, but with a practiced hand, he lowered the flaps and brought the plane down into a smooth water landing, startling a few ducks in the process.

"You could have warned me about the landing," she muttered between clenched teeth.

"Ahh, but then you never would have agreed to come. Besides, why did you think the plane had floats on it?"

"Is it too late to catch a cab home?"

"You could, but I'd bet Über rates for this far out are ridiculous. Now c'mon, we've got a bit of a hike." He grabbed the large camping pack, fishing gear, and twin tents from the small cargo hold in back and took off toward the hills.

"Give me something to carry," Taylor called, chasing after him.

"You can carry the fishing gear," he said, handing her the lightest of the luggage.

"Are you kidding me? I want the tents. Give me the tents," she said, motioning for him to trade her for the heaviest of their gear.

"If you insist."

She made a little grunt as she situated the load and then took off at a quick stride, leaving Noah to follow. He wondered what she was trying so hard to prove—and whether it was to him or to herself.

"You ever been fishing before?" he called from behind her. He had to admit, he was enjoying the view.

"Sure, in streams and creeks and stuff as a kid. I caught this huge catfish once almost half the length of my arm."

He laughed and finally quickened his stride to match hers. "You call that huge?" he asked, coming up beside her. "Wait until you meet the King Salmon. After all, he's king for a reason."

"How about you? Have you been fishing before?" she asked, breaking out into a laugh almost as soon as she'd finished the question.

He turned to stare at her, and she offered him a goofy grin. Having a destination and a plan seemed to put her at ease—or maybe it was just being on solid ground again.

"You know I have," he said as kindly as he could manage.

"Yeah, but how many times?"

"At least a hundred."

"And you hunt larger stuff, too?"

"First, you don't hunt fish. Unless you want me to get you a spear, in which case you should have told me before we left. Second, oh yeah. Hunting is a way of life up here."

Her next question came out as an almost strangled whisper. "Is it hard to kill the animals?"

"No, we do it humanely, and we use every part. Plus, the state department hands out licenses following a quota designed to keep the populations in check. It helps protect the herds year-round and makes sure there is enough to provide for those that are left." He fixed his eyes on her and waited for her to return his gaze. "I wasn't expecting that question from you," he admitted.

Her face scrunched up as if she was having a hard time figuring something out. Finally, she said, "Why not?"

"Because of what you do. You must have had to make peace with the fact that you could take another human life."

"Yeah, but I've never seen combat, and it's doubtful I ever will."

"Does that disappoint you?"

"A little, but I'm also kind of relieved, too. I have very mixed feelings about... well, all of it. The only thing I know for sure is I want to serve my country and help make people's lives better."

"You do seem conflicted."

"About combat? I just told you I am."

"No, about everything. Literally *everything*."

She turned to pout at him, but the expression seemed forced. "Well, that's not very nice."

"It's not meant to be mean or nice. It's just an observation."

"Maybe keep your observations to yourself?"

"Fair enough." When Noah turned to look at her

again, she kept her eyes focused straight ahead. A look of consternation pinched at her face.

She was right, of course.

He *was* pushing her too hard. But then again, it felt so easy to share these things with Taylor. He'd never found himself so intrigued by anyone before, and although he still didn't want to sacrifice himself to the altar of marriage, he had to admit that spending time with Taylor felt good. It felt right.

Maybe because she herself was like a game. Not a conquest, but rather a puzzle. The more time he spent trying to figure her out, the more he craved a solution, an understanding.

One very large question remained...

"Why are you spending time with me?" he asked, dreading the answer. Would she bite back with an insult, or would she finally reveal what was so obviously in her heart?

"Because you asked," she said simply, offering a placating smile as she finally turned to look at him again.

But, no. That answer wasn't enough. Not for Noah.

He took a slow, measured breath before reframing his question. "You've made it clear that you're not afraid to stick up for yourself and you don't do anything you don't want to, so why do you want to be here with me?"

Taylor stopped walking for a second as if his question had ground her to an actual halt. "I don't know. I just do," she said at last.

"Good enough for me," Noah answered with a laugh, turning back to where she stood rooted in place.

And for now, it had to be. He would figure out the rest soon enough.

After all, he had a plan.

Taylor wondered if she'd given away too much by admitting how much she enjoyed spending time with Noah. But it should have been obvious, right? After all, they were here together in the wilderness, and she'd trusted him enough to deliver her safely via that rickety little plane.

"Well, since we've stopped, may as well set up camp," Noah said, motioning for her to hand over one of the tents.

She set to work on the other and asked, "What about fishing?"

"If there's still good light when we're done, we'll head out today. Otherwise, we'll hit it in the morning, bright and early."

She watched his strong arms as he spread out the tent and snapped together the central pole system. Noah caught her looking and smiled, but for once didn't tease her.

And for a moment it all felt so real, as if she were out for the weekend with her boyfriend. In this momentary fantasy, each of them knew how the other felt and had long stopped fighting it. They were in it for the long haul, and above all else, they were comfortable being themselves with each other.

Taylor shook her head to clear the ridiculous daydream from her brain. She didn't even feel comfortable with herself, so how on earth could she ever relax with someone else so completely?

After all, that was another reason for her no dating rule.

Whenever her mother asked about boyfriend prospects, Taylor had told her she'd married the military. She'd said it so often, in fact, that her mother had practically stopped asking. She'd even adopted a hodgepodge of rescue dogs to serve as her pseudo grandchildren.

At first, Taylor had been happy. It would mean

less pestering, but now she realized that her mother had simply given up on her. Was Taylor really such a hopeless case?

Maybe so.

Still, just because she'd met a nice man now, that didn't mean anything had changed. She liked Noah, but they barely knew each other. And she was too much of a pragmatist to remain at her post in Anchorage if another opportunity came along. She had every single reason to leave, and only maybe the whisper of a reason to stay.

She reached down for another piece of the tent, only to realize she'd assembled the full thing while lost in her daydream. She'd even managed to beat Noah who was still finishing up his.

"Good thing that wasn't a contest," he said, slapping his hands together. "Because I lost, big time."

Taylor should have made a joke or even taken a jab at him, although she couldn't help but reflect on his words in light of her recent stream of thoughts.

When the time came, she would leave Anchorage. It wasn't a contest. Not at all.

"Seems I underestimated you. I won't make that mistake again." Noah laughed, and finally, she allowed herself to join him. They were here as friends to have fun. The hard decisions had already been made, whether or not Noah knew it.

"That's right, mister," she answered, grabbing the fishing gear from the spot Noah had dropped it. "Prepare to lose at fishing, too."

Six

They made their way over to the rushing river. Noah had already noticed that Taylor was in better shape than him, but now she was literally walking circles around him.

"Why are you so slow?" she asked, sticking her tongue out as she passed him again.

"Why are *you* so fast?" he countered. "You do know the whole point of fishing is to relax and take things easy?"

She skipped ahead again, and he thought he saw a shrug. "This is me relaxed," Taylor said.

And despite her rapid motions, he believed her. Clearly she'd had some change of heart and it had worked wonders to soothe her anxiety. Did that mean she'd finally given in to her attraction for him?

Well, they would find out soon enough, because he had a plan.

That night, under the stars, with the campfire crackling, he'd ask her if he could kiss her again. It would be the perfect romantic setting, and this time he doubted she'd say no. At least he hoped she wouldn't.

They reached the creek and Noah pulled out his family's trusty old tackle box. Because his father was the last to go fishing, he'd left dozens of pre-tied lures in several small baggies waiting and ready. And almost as quickly as they'd reached the river, they both had poles set up with brightly colored Spin-N-Glo lures.

Taylor studied hers with a serious expression. She was obviously serious about beating him at fishing, as she'd put it. "This looks like one of those helicopter nuts that fall out of trees," she said.

"It kind of is. These spinners twirl in the water," he answered as he showed Taylor the correct way to cast out.

She copied his motions with ease, asking, "And salmon think that looks tasty or something?"

"Nope. It makes them mad," he said as they watched the ripples on the water, then turning toward her with triumph, added, "So mad, in fact, they threaten to break both of its arms."

Taylor jabbed at him, but he moved out of the way just as quickly.

"Save some of that fight for the fish."

They both laughed, then fell into a companionable silence as they waited for something to bite.

"So where are they?" Taylor asked only a few short moments later.

"Who? The fish?"

"Well, yeah. In every show or movie I've ever seen, they're leaping out of the water and into bears' mouths."

"Yeah, you probably watch TV too much. They aren't always jumping, but it makes for a better documentary than watching a bear wade out into the water, duck his head under and then pop back up with a fish in his mouth. Give it a moment. Fishing takes a little skill, a little luck, and a lot of patience. You have to—"

Taylor's cries of joy cut off his speech. "Ooh, oh! I think I caught one!"

Sure enough, her pole bowed as the fish on the end of it tried to swim upstream and out of reach.

"Fish on!" he yelled out. "And a big one, from

the looks of it." He reeled his lure back in and then reached over to help Taylor pull her catch ashore.

"I've got this," she insisted proudly. "I want to catch it myself." She jerked the pole and spun the reel, but the fish's instincts won out over her inexperience.

"What a workout!" she said, theatrically reaching up to wipe her brow and almost losing the pole in the process.

"That's it!" Noah circled his arms around her from behind and added his strength to the fight against the fish. "Can't afford for you to lose our dinner."

He felt her tense in his arms and then relax into his hold. Yeah, she totally liked him back, but like the fish, she was fighting hard to avoid the inevitable.

"Keep the rod tipped up. Let him tire himself out a bit," he mumbled in her ear. "When the pull lets up..."

Almost as if on cue, the tension on the pull eased.

"Okay," he said, widening his stance and instructing her to do the same. "Bring the tip down and start reeling."

She worked the reel frantically, when suddenly, the line started getting dragged back out.

"Bring it back up and hold," he said, helping to transition back to the first position.

"But he's getting away!" she cried, cranking at the reel but not making much progress.

He couldn't help but laugh. Taylor was something else, all right, but one thing was for certain, she was determined to bring this fish home.

"Think of it like tug of war," Noah guided her. "He's going to pull out, then you'll pull in and whoever tires out first, loses."

"I'm not losing," she said with a husky, low voice.

"Oh, I believe you think that. Let's see what actually happens," he teased, smiling when she let out an annoyed sigh.

The fish leaped into the air in a flash of pink and silver.

"There's the jumping you wanted, now reel!" he shouted, but Taylor was already on it.

Twenty minutes later, they'd at last worked the fish into submission and brought it ashore. Noah had guided, but it was Taylor who'd done all the work.

"Oh, my gosh!" she cheered. "We did it!"

"*You* did it," he said, loving how happy she

looked as she studied the fish flopping on the ground. "I was just backup."

"Thank you, Mr. Fish. You will make a very tasty dinner, and I promise I will always remember you fondly."

Noah couldn't control his laughter. "Are you breaking up with him?"

"No, just acknowledging his sacrifice." She remained serious, exhausted, proud as they both studied the fish and how his scales caught and reflected the waning sunlight. "He really is a beauty. How big do you think he is?"

"Oh, forty-five pounds or so. I can get the scale in a minute, but I'm glad you find the fish so attractive, because you're going to have to kiss it."

Taylor put a hand on each hip and glanced over at him in horror. "This isn't the princess and the frog, and you're not funny. Very *not* funny."

"I'm not trying to be funny! I'm serious. Here in Alaska, we fishers have a tradition. You have to kiss your first King, and this guy is yours. Right?" he goaded her, knowing she would rise to the challenge. She was far too competitive not to.

A look of triumph shot across her face as she announced, "We caught him together."

"So you want to kiss him together?"

"It's the only way I can make sure you're being serious here. C'mon, tough guy. Put your mouth where your money is... or something like that."

He slid his hand carefully into the gills of the large salmon and hefted it up, placing his other hand under the tail.

Taylor stepped back as he approached her. "Oh, my gosh, you are being serious, aren't you?"

"Dead serious," he said through laughter he just couldn't contain. "Are you ready?"

She swallowed and took a wide stance, similar to the one she'd used to reel the salmon in. "On three?"

He nodded and started the count, "One."

"Two?" Taylor squeaked.

"Three!"

And just like that, Noah's first kiss with Taylor was on either side of a salmon's face.

He hoped the next one would be far less slimy.

Taylor laughed the whole way back to the campsite. Noah carried their fish and she handled the gear.

"Ready for the best fish dinner you've ever had?" he asked, carefully placing the salmon on a cutting board.

"You know it! Tell me how to help." She crouched down beside him, but he turned away, motioning at a pair of collapsible chairs they'd set up nearby.

"Sit back, keep me company, and I'll handle the rest," Noah said.

"But isn't this the blood, guts, and gore part? I don't want to miss that, seeing as it's the whole reason I came in the first place." She tried to wink at him, but couldn't do so without opening her mouth and pinching the whole right side of her face.

Noah burst out laughing, making her feel self-conscious once again. "I won't ask what that was," he said. "But anyway, you caught. I'll cook. It's only fair."

Taylor decided to give up the fight. Her arms did kind of burn from the earlier workout. Maybe it would be okay to relax for the rest of the evening, build up her strength for the next trip to the river.

She watched in tired awe as Noah deftly gutted, sliced, and seasoned the salmon. By the time the fire had come to a steady blaze, the sky above them had settled on a nice shade of deep red.

"It's beautiful," she said, craning her neck toward the rolling clouds above. She could practically see the colors shifting as the sun continued its descent over the horizon.

Noah poked at the fire before glancing up himself. "Just wait till you see the stars."

"I've seen the stars before, but never a sunset quite like this."

"Trust me. You've never seen stars like this, either. Far away from the city, no light pollution. It's like you can see straight into the heavens." He lowered his gaze on her, and somehow it felt hotter than the fire blazing before her.

"How poetic from a man whose hands are buried deep in fish guts," she joked in an attempt to dial down the sudden intimacy.

He shook his head and laughed. "You never just let it happen, do you?"

She hated that he'd called her out. So instead of acknowledging his question, she looked back up at the skies, pretending to be too distracted to have heard him properly. She didn't know the answer to that particular question anyway.

But he wouldn't let it go. "I know you heard me," Noah said. "You never let things take their natural course, you know? You're just as bad as this fish."

"You gonna debone me, too?" Too late, she realized how wrong that sounded. Heat rushed to her face so quickly it made her dizzy.

"Maybe if you're lucky," Noah teased, returning his attentions to the filets.

"I didn't mean..."

"Relax, I know."

Taylor wrapped her arms around herself as the air cooled. She was also much more careful with her words as they continued their chat beside the campfire. Noah seemed in his element out here in the Alaskan wilderness, but Taylor felt very out of hers. She didn't want a relationship, didn't want romance, and yet here they were with all the makings of the perfect date.

Private plane ride. *Check.*

Beautiful sunset. *Check.*

A freshly prepared meal. *Check.*

Crackling fire. *Check.*

Playful banter. *Check, check, check...*

All the stinking boxes were checked, leaving Taylor to wonder when she had found the time to compile a list.

It felt like it could be easy—being with Noah—if only she were to let it. But how could she?

Taylor was just about to remind him that they weren't on a date, when he flipped a smoky filet onto a tin plate and handed it to her. "Dinner is ready just in time for the show," he told her, pointing above.

And as she glanced up, she nearly dropped her plate in shock.

"Careful," Noah said, catching it for her and coming to sit right at her side with a plate of his own.

"You weren't kidding," she whispered, studying the spectacle above. The sky wasn't even completely dark yet but rather a deep shade of majestic purple. And now millions of stars had come out to shine down on them. The once-in-a-lifetime view of an overlapping sunset and night sky took her breath clear away.

She'd never seen anything like it.

Never met anyone quite like Noah.

It was almost too perfect. But perfect was exactly the thing she didn't need, couldn't want.

"Noah, I..." she started, unsure of what she needed to say and if she had the strength to actually say it.

"What's your sign?" he asked with a lazy smile.

She wanted to make a joke about bad pickup

lines, but doing so seemed disrespectful in the presence of this beautiful display.

"Gemini," she answered. "But I don't believe in astrology."

Noah slid even closer and raised her arm toward the sky, tracing the outline of a faraway constellation. "There they are, the twins. Do you see them?"

He continued to trace the path of the stars over and over until she finally recognized their shape as one she had seen many times—though never in person.

"That's incredible," she said with a slow breath out. "Do you know them all?"

He nodded slowly as he continued to study the stars. "All the zodiac constellations and many more."

"Show me."

Noah reached for her hand again, and her entire body felt as if it were on fire, just like the night sky had been only minutes before. "Libra, the scales. That's my sign."

"Do you know their stories, too?"

"What good boy scout doesn't? Want me to show you my favorite?"

Their entwined hands followed the stars in the path of a W.

"Cassiopeia?" she guessed.

"Yes, that's the queen of the night sky."

"They say she was the most beautiful woman anyone in the world had ever seen." He bumped her shoulder with his. "Kind of like someone else I know."

Noah let go of her hand and reached up to brush aside a strand of hair that had fallen loose from her ponytail. "But unlike you, Cassiopeia knew how beautiful she was and often boasted about it, then there was that whole chaining her daughter to a rock thing, but we don't really need to talk about that."

He chuckled softly, waiting for... something. Something that Taylor just couldn't give.

She took a deep breath, trying to look away, but he stopped her. "Noah, I..."

"I know," he whispered, not bringing his face closer but not pulling away either.

And by the flickering light of the fire, she stared into Noah's eyes and let him see into hers. His eyes flashed brilliantly, not unlike the stars above--and she wondered what he must think of her. Did he really regard her as an other-worldly beauty like Queen Cassiopeia?

And would it really be so bad to let him kiss her, to see where things could go if she stopped holding back?

Noah's face inched closer, and at last she closed her eyes, ready for whatever came next.

MRRRRUAAAAAAHHHHHH!

A terrible cry rent the night sky, ripping Noah and Taylor apart before they could even come together.

Seven

"What was that?" Taylor asked without the slightest hint of fear in her voice. Sure, flying in a perfectly safe plane terrified her, but an attack from a yet-to-be-identified wild animal was business as usual.

The campfire had died down during their stargazing, but their eyes hadn't had time to adjust to the blackness yet.

Taylor jumped to her feet, ready to investigate, but Noah pushed her back to the other side of the campsite. They still didn't know what animal had joined them and what kind of mood it was in, but from the sounds of things, it wasn't good.

"Let me help," she argued.

He pushed her back again. This was one area where he refused to compromise. If anything happened to this poor, city girl, he'd never forgive himself. "No way! I have way more experience in this area. Let me handle it."

That was when another frustrated cry rang out again, and Noah followed the sound cautiously moving toward the animal in distress.

Taylor was right on his heels, refusing to let him deal with the situation on his own.

As they drew closer to the source of the cries, he saw one of the shiny tents jerking about in the sky. The sounds were coming from inside, and he instantly understood.

"It's a moose," he explained to Taylor, pushing ahead of her and using his body as a shield. "Luckily, not a full grown one. He's still a juvenile, which is why he didn't know to stay out of the campsite."

"What happened? What is he doing?" she whispered, looking to him for guidance in her fight against nature once again.

"My guess is one of us forgot to close up the tent properly and he poked his head in. Now he can't get it back out."

"I've never seen a moose up close before," she said in awe.

"And you're not going to now. Seriously, these guys are huge," he hissed, pushing her back yet again. "This one in particular is clumsy and anxious. Not a great recipe for safety."

"But it's dangerous for you, too. Let me help." As she pushed past him again, he realized it would be easier to let her help than to have her force her way into the situation.

"Fine," he grumbled. "Go grab a flashlight and point it at the tent."

As she shone the light on the tent, Noah crept up and grabbed the bottom of the moose's makeshift hat. The gigantic animal thrashed and stomped his feet in frustration as Noah struggled to pull the tent off his head—until, with a rip and snort, the tent fell away in tatters at last.

"Go away, moose! Get out of here!" Noah screamed as loud as he could. Finally, Taylor shrank away, but not for fear of the animal. "Yell with me," he told her, still at full volume. "We need to scare this guy away. Otherwise, he could hurt himself even more, or he could turn on us. Yell with me, Taylor. Yell!"

After a few tense moments, the moose shook his rack, seemingly thankful to have been freed but not anxious to stick around. With all the casual grace of a drunken sailor on land, the moose trotted off on its long knobby legs.

"Whoa, that definitely doesn't happen back home in South Carolina," Taylor said, holding the flashlight under her face so that it made her look like a jack-o-lantern.

"Look at you, catching a salmon, rescuing a moose. You're a real Alaskan now. But I've got bad news for you, Ms. Hunt."

"Uh-oh? Is he coming back just as soon as he finds his little squirrel friend?" she said, breaking into a fit of laughter.

"Just remember, I tried to be a perfect gentleman." Noah groaned as she directed the flashlight toward him, blinding him temporarily. "Yeah, anyway, we're going to have to sleep together. That tent is way too damaged for either of us to take shelter in."

"Excuse me?" she said with a laugh, and he couldn't tell if she was being playful or just really nervous. "But I'm not that type of girl."

"Tonight you are," he said with a shrug. "I promise to be on my best behavior."

"What if the moose comes back?"

"He won't."

"But what if he does?"

"Then I'll keep you safe." He glanced over at Taylor as she raised a hand to each of her hips. "And you can help, too."

Taylor seemed happy enough, but Noah cursed his bad luck. He'd been so close to kissing her until that moose had totally spoiled the mood. Now if he made a move to kiss her, she would think he was trying for more—considering their new sleeping arrangement.

And he wanted all of Taylor Hunt, not just her body. He wanted her heart, her laughter, her smiles... As he watched her rummage through the bag he'd packed for her earlier that day, he finally realized that this wasn't just some simple crush.

He had it bad for this strange new woman who refused to believe him when he told her she was beautiful, who wouldn't stand back and let him take care of her but insisted on taking care of things right alongside him.

Were his feelings for her enough to justify letting her fully into his life? Was she worth the risk to his schedule, to his heart, to his cat's spot on the bed?

"Goodnight, Mr. Nature Guy," she said, patting him on the shoulder before crawling through the opening of their tent and zipping it up behind her.

The answer was a trembling, terrified, emphatic

yes. He didn't know if things between them would come smoothly and naturally or if they'd be more like that clumsy moose who upset their campsite.

But he knew he needed the chance to find out.

🙰

Taylor awoke the next morning, surprised to find she had slept easily through the night. She'd suffered insomnia ever since high school, often waking up several times in the night to tend to whatever anxious thoughts were weighing on her mind.

This morning, though, she'd slept well and felt calm. Taylor *never* felt calm.

Noah still lay sleeping beside her in the cramped tent meant for one. Their bodies had shifted into each other during the night and rather than lying back to back as they'd started out, one of his arms lay draped over her waist. The other was snuggled under her neck, completing their embrace.

She sucked a slow breath in, trying not to disturb Noah as she attempted to make sense of what this all meant. They'd slept in cramped quarters in a popup tent on the ground, and yet she felt as if she'd spent the whole night wrapped in a cloud.

Was she just tired from the big day they'd had or...?

Even finishing that thought scared her.

And why? Why was it this man who had crept stealthily into her heart? She liked Noah a lot—she couldn't deny that any longer—but what made him so danged special?

Why was he worth considering a change to her entire life? To abandoning her no dating, not ever, policy?

She didn't have the answers and somehow doubted she ever would. Perhaps sometimes two people just worked together, just clicked into place like a big spoon and a little spoon nestled snugly in a drawer... or in a tent meant for one.

For a moment, she allowed herself to snuggle into the still sleeping Noah's embrace. She breathed in the scent of him, which was both woodsy and clean. She wondered how different her life would be if she woke up every morning like this, refreshed from a perfect night of sleep, luxuriating in the arms of the man she lo—

Oh, shoot.

This was not part of the plan. And people made plans for a reason. You were supposed to follow through, not abandon them the moment it got hard.

She needed some distance and fresh air to help her think.

Even though she tried her best not to wake Noah as she shifted toward the tent's exit, he roused the moment she was out of his arms.

"Good morning, beautiful Taylor," he said, a contented smile on his face, his eyes still closed shut.

No, no, no. This was way too domestic, way too *un*Taylor.

Then why did it feel so right?

And why was she so confused about it all? Taylor had often felt anxious but was rarely ever confused.

Noah was like a question mark and an exclamation point both rolled into one. What she *needed* was a period. Closure. A return to the plan. The farther she crept from his arms, the more she felt in control again.

"Is something wrong?" he asked, sitting up and placing a hand on her shoulder.

"I'm just not feeling very well," she said, realizing it was only half a lie. "Can we go home?"

"Of course. We can pack up and leave as soon as we've had our breakfast."

"Thank you," she whispered, feeling like the worst person in the world for leading him on, letting him down—and letting herself down, too.

"You stay here and try to rest. I'll get breakfast ready." And before she could argue, Noah had left to prepare another campsite meal for the two of them to share.

As she lay in the tent alone, her brain made up for lost time. All the thoughts that had been missing from her nightly anxiety reel now sped through her head so fast they broke the sound barrier.

So many questions, and the only answer that made any sense was the wrong one.

No to Noah. No to love.

Yes to duty. Yes to the plan.

A short while later, he called her out and handed her a mug with hot cocoa and a plate with eggs and toast. "It should be easy on your stomach," he explained. "Is that what hurts?"

She nodded glumly, attempting to hide her face behind the rim of her mug. Her stomach was filled with both butterflies and dread—definitely not a winning combination.

"I hope it wasn't the fish," he said with a frown, bringing his mug up to take a long, slow sip of the hot liquid inside. She needed to pull away now to avoid hurting him, yet it seemed she already had. Hurt him, that was—and she hated it. Maybe it would be best to just be upfront.

She swallowed hard before saying, "No, Noah. It was great. You're great, but..."

"Oh, I see."

She tried to smile, but couldn't force it, given the circumstances. "I'm sorry."

"You don't need to apologize to me, but I do think you owe it to yourself."

She didn't know what to say to that, so she said nothing.

"What are you so afraid of?"

"I'm not afraid," she answered flatly.

"You weren't afraid of that crazy moose, but you're afraid of this." He turned to her and grabbed each of her shoulders, staring into her eyes as he spoke. "You were afraid of the plane, but you got on it anyway and let it take you where you needed to go. So, why are you afraid of us?"

She still didn't say anything. What could she say? He was absolutely right.

"It's like there are two Taylors, and you've shown me glimpses of the real one, but then you pull back and hide her again under this... this mask. It's the real Taylor that I want to spend time with, and it's the real Taylor who wants me, too."

Noah kept one hand on her shoulder and lifted the other up to tug at her hair tie. As he pulled his hand away, her dark waves cascaded over her shoulders, loose and free. So unlike her normal high and tight ponytail. So unlike her normal composure and control.

"What are you doing?" she whispered, feeling both like she was under scrutiny and that she was finally able to relax and let herself go.

"I'm trying to show you how beautiful you are. The real you," Noah murmured, drawing her eyes to his soft mouth.

She shook her head. "I'm not beautiful."

His lips began to move again, but whatever words he had planned for her never made it out. Without thinking—because she'd already done too much of that already—Taylor pressed her mouth to his and at last, they shared their first kiss.

Eight

～

Noah hadn't expected Taylor to kiss him, but now that she had, he never wanted it to stop. Maybe they could build a little cabin out here by the river and live forever—just the two of them in a perfect, little life.

Taylor pulled back to take a deep, steadying breath, and he saw that his stubble had marked her skin with little red splotches. Her cheeks shone red, too, and her lips.

And he was kissing her again.

She tasted like cocoa and coming home.

"Noah," she whispered against his mouth, leaning her forehead on his and keeping their lips close. Her breath warmed his skin in pleasant, intoxicating puffs.

If this was a game, then he'd definitely won... maybe they both had.

"Noah," she said again.

"Taylor." He leaned in to kiss her again, but she leaned to the side, causing his lips to land on her cheek instead.

"This can't be anything serious," she warned. Her voice was shaky as if trying to conceal a lie—or maybe tears.

"Why not?" he asked, trying in vain to kiss her again.

"I don't date."

"Looks like you do now." He smiled, but her brow remained furrowed with tension.

"No. I'm married to the Army," Taylor said.

"You're getting a little ahead of yourself there. I haven't asked you to marry me. I just want to see where we could go." How could he get through to her, make her willing to accept the risk that always came hand in hand with the best things in life?

"That's the beauty of life," he continued, hoping his words would be enough. "You don't have to know exactly how it will play out in the end. It's getting there that's the exciting part." He reached for both of her hands and laced his fingers through hers. "This is the *exciting* part."

She ducked her head and spoke to him from beneath a veil of lashes. "Noah, I like you. I do, but..."

"Hey, you're the one who kissed me here." He laughed nervously, but she remained serious.

"Maybe that was a mistake."

"No, it wasn't. We're good together, Taylor, even you can't deny that."

She frowned but gave up on arguing any further.

Noah saw this as his chance. Maybe the only chance he would get. "Look, we don't have to decide anything right now, okay? We enjoy each other's company, so let's spend time together. Let me take you out for a date."

"Isn't that kind of what this is right now?" She looked back at him. Her eyes said everything her lips refused to let pass.

"I want to take you for a real one with flowers and dinner, holding open doors and pulling out chairs."

Taylor frowned again and sucked in a deep breath.

Noah hurried to fill the brief silence before she could officially reject his proposal. "Well, I didn't say who would be pulling out chairs and opening doors. You're welcome to treat me, if that's what you want."

He laughed softly and leaned in to kiss her again. This time, she didn't resist. "Is that a yes?"

She looked away again. "That's a yes to seeing where things can go, but I still don't have a lot of hope here."

"Well, then I'll have enough hope for both of us. Agreed?"

Turning back, she asked, "Why do you like me so much?"

"Hey, if memory serves, I asked you that question already and you refused to answer it with anything more than 'because.'"

She pouted her big, beautiful lips, and Noah had to fight the urge to kiss her again. "Does that mean you won't tell me?"

"I've already told you dozens of times by now, but I will happily tell you again. Taylor, you're beautiful, brave, smart, and funny. You challenge me, make me fight for you... and with you. Things haven't been boring for even a single second. I never knew I could meet someone like you, but now that I have, I can't let you get away without at least giving me a chance."

She finally smiled. "It sounds like you had that prepared." She was teasing him, but at least she was smiling. Taylor's smile had become his very favorite thing in the whole world.

"There you go again," he said with a laugh. "Never a dull moment. Never easy. But here's the thing: everything else in my life is easy already. Well, except for my cat... I like that you make things difficult."

She laid her head on his shoulder as they continued to talk. "If this is supposed to win me over, you're doing kind of a bad job here."

"The difficult things are the ones that mean the most." He swept his fingers through her hair, luxuriating in the intimacy of the moment. "Taylor, you give my life this whole new layer of meaning that wasn't there before. You keep me guessing. You—"

"You complete me?" She laughed so hard, both their bodies shook.

"Okay, so maybe I'm straying into sappy territory. I'm new at this, too, you know."

"At dating?"

"Yeah, actually. I had a no relationships rule, same as you."

"I never would have guessed that with how hard you seem to try every moment we're together, even from that first day in the store."

"Like I said, I enjoy a challenge."

One by one, Taylor poked her fingers through the spaces between the buttons on his flannel shirt. "Am I still a challenge now that I've agreed to go on a date with you?" she asked.

"Probably even more so now."

"What do you mean?"

"Well, we've leveled up. The higher levels are always the hardest."

She laughed and dropped both her hands into her laugh. "I don't even know what you mean anymore."

"You don't like my tortured metaphor?" He laughed and picked up her hands, squeezing them in his. "Then let me give it to you straight. Taylor Hunt, I'm going to make you fall in love with me."

Taylor tensed against him, and Noah felt happy he couldn't see whatever tortured expression crossed her face. "And I'm not going to let you do that," she warned.

"Taylor, don't you see?" He tilted her face toward his, making sure she looked into his eyes as he said, "In this game, we can both win. *Together.*"

Taylor clutched onto her seatbelt for dear life. It wasn't the flying that scared her this time, but rather everything else.

Kissing Noah. Not kissing him.

Staying in Anchorage. Leaving for good.

She felt hopelessly stuck, like neither option was right for her anymore.

He dropped her off at the hangar and promised to pick her up for their big date Wednesday night at seven o'clock. That, at least, gave her a few days to screw her head on straight, regain her focus, decide what he meant to her.

And in the days that followed, her mind continued to drift to Noah. She caught little precious sleep, and when she did manage it, she dreamt of him, too. There was no escape. How could she both crave and dread something at the same exact time?

After a slow and agonizing start to the week, Wednesday finally arrived. Maybe their date would bring her clarity. And who knew?

Maybe once she saw him again, she'd realize that all the feelings were already gone. She could have built this whole thing up in her head, simply for something to distract herself from the perpetual boredom that had come with her posting in Anchorage.

She ran a brush through her hair, debating whether to keep it down the way Noah liked it or to pull it up into her tight regulation ponytail. After a ridiculous amount of stalling, she settled on a half and half do.

Taylor owned exactly one dress, and she pulled it on over her head now. The simple, black fabric felt weightless against her skin. Her legs, arms, and collar bone were all exposed, making her feel naked, on display.

And she didn't have any fancy shoes to pair with the outfit—plus, she refused to wear nylons—so she slipped a pair of black flats onto her bare feet and called it good enough.

Even though her dressed-up look was still pretty tame, Taylor felt like an awkward imposter. Why had Noah insisted on taking her to the kind of restaurant that required reservations? She'd much rather head to McDonald's, if it meant she could wear her favorite jeans and a T-shirt.

Noah arrived a short while later, leaving Taylor grateful that she hadn't gotten any additional alone time with the makeup collection her mother had gifted her a couple Christmases back. Her face was blissfully bare, and her skin could breathe... even though her lungs had a hard time bringing in enough air.

"You look..." Noah said as he led her to his car idling at the curb.

"Beautiful?" she mumbled. After all, that was his favorite word for her.

"*Uncomfortable*," he said, stopping outside of the car without unlocking the doors for either of them. "Don't get me wrong. You look beautiful, too, but I'm guessing you don't much care for wearing dresses."

"It's fine," she argued. The sooner they got on with their date, the sooner she could come home and change into her nice, familiar casual wear again.

"No, it's not," Noah insisted with a firm shake of his head. "Look, I chose this place because they make the best prime rib you've ever tasted—and that's a promise, by the way. But we don't need to put on any kind of show. I want you to enjoy yourself."

She crossed her arms over her chest, feeling even more awkward now that Noah had called her out. "I can't exactly wear jeans to a five-star restaurant."

"No, but we can order takeout. Go get changed, and I'll call the restaurant to let them know our order will be to go."

That did sound nice, but it also sounded like too much trouble.

"Noah, it's fine. Really. You don't need to change the plans on my account."

He laughed softly and shook his head. "Yes, I do. I may not be an expert, but I know enough to know that when a woman repeatedly tells you something is fine, that means it's not. And like I said, I want you to have a good time. So please go, go change. Let me take care of the rest."

Noah locked his car, and the two of them returned to her apartment door. After letting them both in, she went straight to her bedroom and put on her off-duty uniform of jeans and a T-shirt. And that simple change made her feel like herself again—the real Taylor Noah had told her about, the one that lived beneath the mask.

She listened through the door as Noah spoke with the restaurant staff and placed their order to go. How had Noah known she would be miserable the entire night without a quick change up? Even her mother still hadn't figured this out about her.

"Everything okay in there?" Noah called after hanging up with the restaurant.

"Sure is!" she shouted back, deciding to apply a little eyeshadow and mascara after all. This man was willing to adjust to meet her needs, yet she'd so rigidly insisted that they could never work. Maybe the work that needed to be done wasn't on them, but rather on herself.

Noah had said that she never just let anything happen.

Maybe this time she could.

Maybe Noah would have his way after all. Because the more time she spent with him, the more she believed that she really could fall in love.

That one day, she could even end up as somebody's wife.

As Noah's.

Nine

Noah waited in Taylor's sparsely decorated living room while she changed into something more comfortable. Normally, he loved the sight of a beautiful woman all dressed up, especially if it was for a date with him.

But Taylor had just looked miserable. Now that he knew how infectious her smile could be, he wanted to do everything he could to make sure it never faded.

He was still in awe of what an incredible woman Taylor had turned out to be. He never would have guessed that their simple flirtations at the electronics store could lead to so much more. And he meant it when he said that he was going to make her fall in love with him. He was already falling—falling so fast, it excited and terrified him in equal measures.

Good thing he had always loved a good thrill rush.

As for Taylor, she'd given so much to their country, though she seemed to belittle her sacrifice since she hadn't yet seen combat. Still, she was fraught with anxiety over every little decision and non-decision alike. She deserved to smile. She deserved to finally be able to relax and know that someone was taking care of her, too—that she didn't have to do it all on her own as she always had.

Oh, he had it bad.

Perhaps he'd caught the love bug from his brother, Oscar. As much as the goofy, lovesick version of his brother irritated him, he also realized now that he'd been a bit jealous of that happiness.

And now he also knew why.

Finding a girl you wanted to risk everything for made life so much fuller. Maybe even ornery Billy Idol would come around to Taylor in time. They could be one big happy family, and...

Okay, he needed to calm *way* down.

This was their first official date, and the last thing he needed to do was ruin it with ridiculous declarations of love. They didn't even know each other well enough, though it kind of did feel like he'd seen straight into her heart that weekend on their fishing trip.

And it kind of did feel like she was finally beginning to see into his.

Just then, the door to Taylor's bedroom opened from inside, and she strode across the living room to join him on the couch. "Sorry it took so long," she said.

"That's okay. You're worth waiting for." And he meant that in every sense of the word.

He wanted to lean in and kiss her again. Not kissing her these past few days had been a new and unwelcome form of torture, but he wanted her to make the next move. He needed to know that she was comfortable, that he wasn't rushing her along too fast.

Or like a startled moose, she could run away and never look back.

Noah didn't want to be just some guy she'd known once. He wanted to be *the* guy, and the fact that didn't send him running straight out that door seemed nothing short of a miracle.

Or some kind of divine destiny.

"Did you order the food?" Taylor asked, folding

her hands in her lap and looking up at him shyly from behind freshly painted eyes.

"It should be ready in about 45 minutes. They'll call."

The phone rang a few seconds later, but it wasn't Noah's. It was Taylor's.

"Well, that was fast," she joked, frowning as she clicked to answer the call. "Hello?"

Noah watched as Taylor listened to the mumbled words of the caller on the other end of the line.

Her eyes widened, and the mumbled stopped. "Just one moment, please."

"Is everything okay?" Noah asked, sensing the tension that rolled off from her in waves.

She smiled, but he didn't buy it. "Yeah, yeah, of course. I just need to take this in the other room."

Worry overtook Noah as he watched Taylor walk away from him for the second time that evening. Why did it feel like she wouldn't be coming back this time?

T aylor closed the door behind her, making sure it had latched all the way. "I'm sorry, could you just repeat all that again, please?" she asked Johnson, one of the Call of Duty guys that worked with her.

"Let's just say I was passing by a desk and happened to see your name on some paperwork. Looks like your transfer request has been approved. Unit Supply Specialist in Charleston. Congrats, Hunt."

"I'm sorry, did you say Charleston?" She couldn't believe it. Almost didn't want to.

"Yes, Hunt. You're headed home."

"Th-thanks, Johnson," she mumbled at last, and they both hung up.

Taylor stared at the idle phone in her hands. She'd gotten her first choice of assignment, a dream come true. So why did it feel like it was somehow a punishment?

And how would she tell Noah?

Panic rose to her chest, and Taylor forced herself to take deep, steadying breaths. Unlocking her phone, she then flipped to her text messages and re-read the last several she'd exchanged with Noah.

I can't wait to see you tonight, he'd texted earlier that day. *Prepare for the best steak of your life!*

And "I'll make you fall in love with me," he'd said after their first kiss.

Only moments ago, she'd decided that maybe—

just maybe—she could love Noah Rockwell. She could change her rules, if it meant getting to keep him by her side.

But tonight's call had come as a firm reminder. Taylor's life wasn't her own. She wasn't the one who got to make the rules. She'd married the military, and now they needed her to move on to some place new.

Was this a reminder, a divine intervention from the almighty General in the sky?

Taylor didn't know about that, but she did know that she had to comply with orders. Whether it came tomorrow or next week, her time with Noah was up.

She would allow herself this one evening, and then she would move on. Soon Noah would be nothing more than a fond memory. Knowing that freed her from her anxieties at last.

Perhaps she could have loved Noah as he so adamantly insisted, but they would never know now.

Next time, she would be more careful. She would guard her heart more closely. She would wear her mask and refuse to let anyone lower it from her face.

Her face! Oh gosh, was that a tear?

She took several more deep breaths, then patted on a bit of powder from her makeup kit to cover the splotchy trails of her sorrow.

"It could have been so much worse," she told herself. "The call came right on time."

She smiled at herself in the mirror. It didn't look authentic. She didn't feel authentic. Noah needed her to be happy, to enjoy the evening. She would let him down later, but he'd already ordered their dinner. They were already here together.

She just needed to find a way to say goodbye.

Ten

oah didn't trust the smile on Taylor's face. It seemed too big, too forced, not like the authentic moments of joy her face had captured during their weekend fishing trip together.

She was hiding something, something related to that call.

"Everything okay?" he asked when she returned to sit beside him on the couch.

"Better than okay," she answered perkily, leaning in to give him their first kiss of the evening.

Noah loved kissing Taylor, but not if she was using their affection as a mask for dishonesty. As hard as it was, he pushed her away and searched her eyes for some seed of the truth.

"Why are you looking at me like that?" She pouted, and a blush rose to her cheeks.

Studying her more closely, he recognized the tell-tale sign of tears, which she'd poorly tried to cover up with some kind of cosmetic cream or powder.

"You're making me uncomfortable," she said, shifting her gaze to the floor, trying to escape him all of a sudden. From awkward to happy to fake to scared, he just couldn't keep up with her shifting moods tonight.

Noah hadn't done anything wrong, which could only mean...

"Am I leaving, or are you?" he whispered.

Taylor jerked her head up to look at him again, that same overzealous smile spread across her face again. But it wasn't the smile he'd come to crave. This wasn't the real Taylor. "No, no, we're both staying here for dinner. You did place the order, right?"

He sighed. Of course, she would be just as difficult as ever. She didn't know any other way to be. "The call," he said, his throat dry as he forced out each word. "It changed something."

"Stop being ridiculous, Noah. Can't we just enjoy tonight?" she begged.

"Taylor, I have always been honest with you, right from the start. Tell me what happened."

She shook her head, smiled. "Noth—"

"And don't you say *nothing*, because I can tell." He placed a hand on her arm and felt her shiver against his palm.

"I am," she said at last.

He nodded even though he didn't understand yet, didn't know which of his questions she had finally decided to answer.

"I'm leaving," she whispered, turning her eyes back toward him. Her tears had begun to fall again, and Noah wanted so badly to kiss them away.

"Was it something I did to make you uncomfortable?" he asked, fearing her answer.

She shook her head sadly. "I put in for a transfer before I even met you, and it just got approved."

"A transfer to where?"

"Charleston."

"When are you leaving?" Now that he knew what he was up against, he needed to know all the details, so that maybe they could find a way through this newest obstacle. Oh, but it was a big one.

"I don't know. It could be tomorrow. It could be several weeks. The Army is a whole lot of hurry up and wait when it comes to these things."

"But you're not leaving tonight?"

She shook her head subtly. "No."

"Then let's make it a night to remember."

Her eyes widened, almost as if she was having a hard time taking in the sight of him—that she couldn't see him clearly, but she wanted to. "How?"

"I don't know yet, but we'll figure it out as we go."

"I don't know, Noah." She shivered again, but didn't resist when he wrapped her in a hug. Instead, she brought her arms up to embrace him, too. Then she whispered, "Won't that just make things harder?"

"They're already hard, and you're already here. Please just give me the night."

"Okay."

Taylor let Noah hold her hand as they walked along the coastal trail following the path outlined by the Anchorage Planet Walk. After finishing their takeout dinner, which was every bit as delicious as Noah had promised, they drove their cars over to a place called the Kincaid Chalet.

"What are we doing here?" she'd asked.

"Leaving," he said, opening the passenger side door to his car and motioning for her to get in. "We'll be back for it soon. Well, *soon-ish*. I promise."

He drove downtown and parked his car in an open lot. He pointed to a huge, yellow dome down the road and told her about the plans he had for them that evening. "We're going to start at the sun and walk all the way to Pluto. The Planet Walk was planned to scale with the solar system. I haven't done it since I was a kid, but I just knew we had to come here tonight."

"And we're going to walk all the way back to where we left my car? That will take forever."

"*If only*," he answered with a sad smile. "It will take us about five hours, but it's our last night together, and I wanted to make sure you'll remember the guy you met back in Anchorage when you're out kicking Army butt in South Carolina."

"And you chose the planets because—"

"Because we already had the stars." Noah tugged at her hand, giving it a tight squeeze as he did. "Now c'mon."

As he guided Taylor gently through Anchorage, he told her stories about all the places they passed.

He'd lived a full life here, brimming with happy memories.

"So, my mom and dad used to try to give us some culture, which meant we spent a lot of time here at the Performing Arts Center." He pointed to the big building opposite the sun installation. "We'd sneak out of concerts and plays when our parents weren't watching and whitewash each other. It was usually Sebastian that got tossed in a snowbank since he was the youngest. When the concerts were over, Mom and Dad would come to find us and we would hide. All of us dressed to the nines, shivering, dripping wet, and out of breath. We usually got grounded after that, but then a few months later, my parents would want to try to culture us again, and we'd act out again. They never gave up trying, though."

Taylor laughed as she pictured it. "It must have been so nice growing up with brothers. Your poor mom, though. Seems like the three of you were really a handful."

"Don't feel too bad for my mom. She's gotten her revenge a hundred times over now that we're grown. I'm kind of sad that she didn't get the chance to meet you, though. She would have loved you."

"Really? Why is that?" Taylor tried to picture what

Noah's mom might look like. Was she tall and heavy like her—or was she petite and pretty? Did she try to force her sons into some kind of mold they'd never fit, or did that all end with their trips to the concert hall?

"Don't worry about that," he said. For the first time since she'd met him, Noah flushed with embarrassment. "Look, we've reached the next planet and the Hotel Captain Cook, named for the famous explorer. Sebastian wanted to be him so much when we were younger, so naturally, Oscar and I ruined it for him by pretending to be the Hawaiians that killed him. Most kids played cowboys and Indians, but not us." It seemed he'd decided that, since they couldn't share their futures, they might as well share their pasts.

"Sounds like you tortured Sebastian growing up," Taylor answered, laughing.

"Believe me, he deserved it. And still does. Didn't you fight with your brothers and sisters?"

"Nope. It was just me and my mom," she told him.

"Your dad?" he asked, looping an arm over her shoulder as a chill rippled through the air.

"Killed in combat before I was born," she told him without feeling any sadness or longing for her father. His absence had always been a fact of life, and she'd never known things any other way.

Noah kissed her temple as they continued to walk slowly forward. "And that didn't put you off joining the Army yourself?"

"No, it's actually a big part of why I decided to enlist. It makes me feel close to him, like I'm carrying on his legacy. He was a brave man."

"And you're an incredible, brave woman," he said, kissing her again.

"And you're too much," she retorted, reaching him to give him a playful jab on the shoulder.

Noah grabbed her wrist and pulled her into his chest. His eyes shone in the setting darkness as he said, "And you're exactly the right amount." Then he kissed her, right there beside Saturn.

"Look, the stars are starting to come out," Taylor murmured, pushing herself out of his embrace. She didn't want to pull away, but if she wasn't strong now, they'd both end up rooted there to that spot well into the morning... possibly forever.

Love wasn't in the cards for Taylor, but—oh—if it was...

She grabbed Noah's hand and tugged him up the trail. If they focused on walking, on the map, then maybe the impending goodbye wouldn't hurt so badly.

"There she is." Noah pointed into the stars above. "Your twin."

Taylor's eyes moved up the length of Noah's arm and into the night sky where she saw a bold, beautiful *W* shining dully. "Cassiopeia."

"Think of me whenever you see her." He stopped walking and wrapped his arms around her. "We'll always have the stars," he whispered, bringing his face close.

"And now the planets, too."

"The whole universe."

They continued the hike in stops and starts, taking their time to appreciate nature's spectacle and their last blissful moments of togetherness.

When they finally reached the Kincaid Chalet, Taylor knew that this was goodbye. There was nothing left to say.

"Don't go yet," Noah said as she glanced toward her car.

"Don't you need a ride back to your car downtown?"

"No, I'll call my brother. I owe him a rude awakening anyway."

"Do you want to go inside?"

"No, it's closed."

"Then?"

"Here, hand me the keys."

Noah opened the driver side door of Taylor's sedan and jammed the key into the ignition, then turned on the radio where some poppy song broadcast into the night.

"I was kind of hoping it would be 'Fly Me to the Moon.' How perfect would that have been?" Noah said, opening his arms and asking Taylor to walk into them for the last time.

"It's already perfect," she said, finally letting down all her defenses, finally trusting herself enough now that it was too late.

Eleven

N oah watched Taylor drive away from the Kincaid Chalet, from him and any life they might have had together. When her tail lights at last disappeared into the night, he sank down onto the stone steps outside the closed building and looked up at the stars.

This is it, he told himself. *Time to move on. What other option do I have?*

There were no solutions, not to this problem. He smiled to himself when he glanced down at his phone and realized the time. At least he had an opportunity to get a little bit of revenge on Sebastian for waking him up early a couple weeks back. He tapped on his brother's contact and waited for the inevitable fight. At least that would take his mind off Taylor—or so he hoped.

"There better be a fire," Sebastian grumbled, the sound of sleep mangling his voice on the other end of their call.

"I need you to come pick me up."

Sebastian groaned. "Okay, be there in a few hours."

"Do I need to set a fire? Because I'll set a fire."

His brother groaned again. "Where are you? Where's your car?"

"I'm at the Kincaid Chalet. My car is not. Now can you come pick me up?" The cold was starting to seep in, and he just wanted to get home and in bed. Sleep off the sadness of loss, maybe.

But Sebastian was stubbornly standing in his way. "This is about that girl, isn't it?" his little brother asked. "The one you stood me up hunting for."

Noah sighed, feeling so very tired now. "Will you just come? Please?"

Sebastian muttered something under his breath as he hung up the phone, but Noah missed it. His brother would come. He had to. As much as they liked giving each other a hard time, they were a tight knit family and were always there for each other when it really counted.

Like now.

Taylor's absence already stung his poor, tired heart. Would time really heal this wound, or would he be stuck for life with a giant, festering wound?

He watched the stars drift across the sky and could have sworn he saw Taylor's smile there among them. Well, this was just perfect. He'd been a perfectly happy, perfectly normal guy—and now he was a sad, sappy victim of love. The only thing worse than allowing himself to fall, of course, was that he'd had nowhere to land.

A short while later, a pair of headlights illuminated Noah on the steps, partially blinding him in the process. Sebastian's big red truck honked at him and drove dangerously close before pulling to a stop.

Noah climbed into the passenger side, expecting a string of curses or at least a good solid ribbing, but instead his little brother stayed silent, driving them both back toward the city.

After several silent minutes passed, Sebastian said, "Tell me about her."

"There's nothing to tell."

"Obviously there is or I wouldn't be picking you up from the boonies in the middle of the night. Did she really drive you out here to, like, literally dump you and leave you behind? That's cold."

"No, she wouldn't do that." Noah rested his head against the window, but Sebastian refused to let him rest.

"Yet here we are. You don't need to make excuses for her."

Noah sighed. "Can we not?"

"Look, you're the one who brought me into this. At least talk to me enough to keep me awake while I drive you home. What was her name?"

"Taylor."

Sebastian chuckled softly, making it obvious he was pretty tired right then, too. "Like Taylor Swift?"

"She'd probably break both of your arms if she heard you make that comparison," Noah answered with a small, sad smile.

"So she's not a girly girl then."

"She's the furthest thing from it you could possibly imagine." Noah sighed wistfully, picturing Taylor in his mind's eye. Her smile. The fact that he would never see it—or her—again.

"Okay, why'd she dump you?" Sebastian made a sharp right turn and Noah slid closer to the window.

"She didn't," he answered.

Sebastian gave his signature groan. "Just tell me."

"Oh, yes, I'm convinced. Let me just pour my heart out to you now."

"Seems like you need to tell someone, and seeing as I'm the only one here. Start talking."

Noah closed his eyes. "She didn't dump me. She has to move. End of story."

"You're just as bad as Oscar, you know that? Worse, actually. Because while he's happy, you're sitting here moping."

Suddenly, Noah just couldn't take it anymore. He was happy that his brother had come to pick him up in the middle of the night, but now that they were together, Sebastian was only rubbing salt into already painful wounds. "What do you want me to do about it?" he shouted.

"Calm down, bro," Sebastian said smoothly. "I don't know the first thing about love or whatever it is you've caught here. All I know is if I met a woman who got under my skin the way this one has so obviously gotten under yours, I wouldn't let her go for anything."

"You're right. You don't know anything," Noah grumbled, returning his voice to its normal volume.

And neither did Noah, as it turned out. He thought that if he wanted it bad enough, things would work out with Taylor. He thought that it was okay to abandon his no relationships rule for the right person. But Taylor obviously hadn't been right, or she wouldn't be going away.

All he knew now is that he had made the wrong choice when it came to Taylor Hunt, and now everything hurt.

He was also determined that he would never make such a stupid mistake again.

Taylor had a hard time driving away from Noah that night. She'd finally admitted that love could fit into her life, only to have it torn away mere seconds later. And now she wished she had never come to Anchorage in the first place, never met Noah, never knew life could be any different.

Yet here she was, driving home at four in the morning, knowing that work would be brutal the next day and not even caring. Noah had told her that the days were about 117 days long on Venus. Well, they were far too short here on Earth.

Life was too short to miss even a moment being afraid. Yet she had wasted almost all of their time together—worrying, wondering what if, being afraid.

Nothing had ever scared Taylor quite as much as the new feelings that rose within her whenever Noah was near. Except for the equally new feelings of dread and loss that flooded that same chest cavity now.

She'd be going home to Charleston, a fact that should make her feel happy. Yet here she was retreating into herself once more, feeling as if she'd let the real Taylor out only to allow her heart to be broken.

Stupid feelings.

She tried to stop thinking of what she could have had with Noah and instead focus on what she did have with the Army. Even though she'd been bored in Anchorage, she loved her job, loved serving her country, carrying on her father's legacy.

She needed to focus on the pride she felt whenever she put on her uniform, the deep fulfillment that came with waking up every day knowing she would make a difference in the defense of her country. Those were the feelings that meant something. Those were the ones that mattered.

Taylor slept easy that night despite her anxiety. She was just too wrung out to stay up any later with her thoughts.

The next morning, she received the details of her transfer. She'd be leaving for Charleston in less than two weeks, which left her just enough time to wrap things up with her life here before moving on to her life there.

And neither life could include Noah. She knew that now. In fact, she'd always known, but sometimes you ignored the truth when it painted a picture you didn't want to see.

She passed her time by playing the video games Noah had recommended to her. They kept her hands and her mind busy, but her heart only ached harder. Why did everything remind her of him?

Play a video game, think of Noah.

Eat fish for dinner, think of Noah.

Look up at the night sky, think of Noah.

Wonder about her future, think of Noah.

This was why Taylor had clung so tightly to the rules. The rules kept people from getting hurt.

So then why did she want to throw them all out the window and run to see Noah one last time before she left Anchorage forever?

Maybe if she just drove by once? Maybe if she just said hello quickly? Could it be enough to clear any thoughts of Noah from her mind once and for all?

And now that she had this idea, she couldn't put it out of her head. She hopped in her car and headed toward his apartment complex, praying that one last glimpse of Noah would solve everything.

She flew up the stairs, having convinced herself now that one last kiss was what she needed. Just one last kiss.

She knocked on his door softly at first, then urgently—so full of need she wanted to burst.

But if Noah was there, he didn't answer. She waited and waited, but he never came.

Defeated, she finally headed back home. This was right. It was what needed to happen. *Maybe it was all in your head, Taylor. Maybe he never loved you back. Maybe he's already moved on.*

She didn't know. She would never know.

And that would have to be okay.

Twelve

⌒꙰⌒

Noah had wanted to stay at home, to see if maybe—just maybe—his cat would take pity on him and actually offer some comfort for his stupid, broken heart.

But missing the weekly family dinner would mean more questions than he was prepared to answer. It was better just to go and hope nobody besides Sebastian noticed how sad the oldest Rockwell brother felt.

"I made your favorite!" his mother said as she hugged him at the doorway. "Prime rib with twice baked potatoes."

"That's great, Mom. Thanks." He forced a smile, hoping it looked genuine.

Nothing ever escaped his mother, though.

"Sebastian mentioned you were feeling down, but didn't say why."

"Did he, now?" Noah was going to kill his baby brother.

"Kelly, he just got here." Thankfully, Noah's father, Wayne, came to his rescue. "Let him come in and relax a bit before giving him the third degree" he mumbled as he ushered his wife back into the kitchen.

Inside the house, Oscar and Lolly sat on the sofa, flipping through old family albums.

"Hi, Noah," his sister-in-law, Lolly, said as she gave him a pitying look. "Sebastian said you weren't feeling too good today."

"So I hear," Noah grumbled. Yup, he was definitely going to kill him. "Speaking of Sebastian, where is the little brat?"

"He had to run to the store for some sour cream for Mom," Oscar answered, studying his brother from across the room. "Tell us what's going on."

But Lolly placed a hand on her husband's arm and gave him a stern look. "Don't force him, Oscar. If he doesn't want to tell us, he doesn't have to."

Noah nodded, and thanked God for bringing Lolly into their lives, seeing as she was the only one who understood enough to leave him be. "Good, because I *don't* want to talk about it, and Sebastian shouldn't have told you all about her."

"Her?" Oscar and Lolly asked in unison.

"Crap," Noah stood, trying to figure out the best escape route. If Sebastian had already aired his business to everyone, then he was in store for an entire night of questioning and unsolicited advice. No, thank you.

"Nope, you're not getting away that easy." Oscar rushed over and pushed Noah back toward the couch. "Who is she? When can we meet her?"

"It doesn't matter, because she's gone."

"Gone as in dead?" Lolly asked, a startled expression on her face.

"No!" Noah didn't even want to think about something that horrible. It was bad enough they were separated now, but at least she could still have a good, full life with the Army—and maybe eventually some other guy.

Oscar plopped onto the couch beside Noah and smiled at him. "Then you've still got a chance."

"You don't even know the circumstances. How could you possibly say that?"

"We don't need to know the particulars. Love always finds a way," Lolly said sagely. "That's why I wrote a song about it."

"I thought I had lost Lolly, too," Oscar reminded them. "She was on her way out to Nashville, but she stayed."

"Well, Taylor's not going to stay, okay? It's impossible."

"Then why can't you go?" Oscar asked, but Lolly hushed him.

She came over to sit beside Noah on the other end of the sofa and grabbed both of his hands in a sisterly gesture. "Noah, listen to me. I've been where you are. When I gave it all up, I gained everything. Do you understand? I thought I knew what I needed to be happy, but then I met your brother and all my other dreams came true, too. That's the funny thing about love—it makes everything better."

Noah sighed. He knew Lolly was right, and he knew his brothers were only pestering him because they cared, but none of that made the situation any easier. "My life was good enough already. It didn't need to be better."

"Yes, but how is it now? You look miserable," she asked softly.

"Lolly, could we please just drop this?"

"We won't force you to do anything," Oscar said, standing and walking back over to the other side of the room. "Anyway, I'm willing to bet that you already know what to do. You're just being a stubborn jerk about it."

Noah laughed bitterly. Oscar was right. He did already know. He knew that it was over, that things were impossible now that Taylor was moving thousands of miles away from him. There was nothing he could do. *The end.*

One month later

Taylor's doorbell rang bright and early on a Saturday morning, the one day she had hoped to sleep in. Knowing that she would never buy from such a tactless door-to-door salesperson or convert to a new religion outside her doorstep, she decided to ignore it and go back to bed.

But the bell continued to ring, and ring... and ring.

Finally, she flung her covers off, tugged on a fleece robe, and went to answer the door. She was greeted by a large green and pink plant.

"Good morning, beautiful!" Noah cried, lowering the potted plant so that she could see his face. "I was beginning to think you'd never answer the doorbell, and I hated the idea that I might have to break in."

"Noah, what are you doing here?" she asked. Already tears had begun to form in the corners of both eyes. She still thought of the man she'd left behind in Anchorage constantly. She longed for him in the day and dreamed about him at night.

And now he was here. *Here!*

He smiled casually as if this were just any old visit between friends. They both knew that it was so much more, though. "I heard you were new in town, so I brought you this plant as a house-warming."

"It's lovely, but—"

"It's a galaxy magnolia. Get it? Like the planets and stars?" He winked and leaned in to kiss her cheek.

"I do, but—"

"And it's not just any plant, it's a tree," Noah continued, immune to her arguments.

"How very thoughtful, but—"

"But? But you want to know what I'm doing here?"

"Don't get me wrong. I'm thrilled to see you, but—"

"But Charleston is a long way from Anchorage?"

"Yes, that."

"Well, you see, I came to deliver the magnolia and to ask you if you know of any good places to grab breakfast around here. Do you?"

"Come inside and I can make you something. You must be famished after your long flight."

"Nah, it only took about ten minutes to get here, actually," he said, following her inside and setting the magnolia down on the kitchen counter.

She stared at him, unable to comprehend what he was trying to tell her, but still so, so happy to see him.

He wrapped his arms around her and pulled her in close. "Okay, I see you're confused."

"Just a little." But being confused was just fine if it meant that somehow, quite impossibly, they could be together.

He kissed her then, just a quick peck that left her wanting so much more. "You remember when we first met?"

She nodded, hoping he would kiss her again now. "Yeah, at the electronics store."

"Which has over two thousand locations nationwide." He smiled so wide, it almost felt as if his grin would fall off the edges of his face. "Well, I put in for a transfer, too."

And, finally, it was all beginning to make sense.

But still, Taylor's heart couldn't believe it. "Did you really move all the way across the country... for me?" she squeaked.

"Something like that."

"But Noah, we haven't known each other that long. What if it doesn't work out? You'll have left everything behind."

"So what?" He raked his hands through her hair, which she hadn't had time to tie back before answering the door. "It's the scariest things that are the most worth trying. I want to be with you, Taylor Hunt, plain and simple."

She closed her eyes, living for that moment. His touch. His words. She never wanted it to end.

Then Noah asked, "Do you want to be with me, too?"

"Yes."

"Then kiss me already. I'm dying over here waiting."

She could have argued. She could have pointed out that they'd already kissed several times since reuniting, but instead, she brought her lips to his. And they shared the first kiss of the rest of their lives, the kiss that would mark the beginning of whatever came next.

"How do you feel?" Noah asked when they parted to catch their breath.

"Beautiful," Taylor answered, kissing him again.

Are you ready to meet Noah's cousin? Charlie is a free spirit, but she accidentally just adopted a big dog with a traumatic past. Can the nerdy guy at the dog park help?

CLICK HERE to get your copy of *In Love with the Nerd*, so that you can keep reading this series today!

And make sure you're on Melissa's list so that you hear about all her new releases, special giveaways, and other sweet bonuses.

You can do that here: MelStorm.com/gift

What's Next?

Charlie Rockwell has always believed in taking life one day at a time. But when she sees a sad-eyed Rottie on TV, she just knows she has to rescue him. Now, Charlie doesn't know how to be a dog-owner, and her new canine companion has even less of an idea how to be a pet. Will the handsome man at the dog park with the well-behaved golden retriever be able to help them turn things around? Add in a few stolen kisses and a life-or-death encounter at a national park, and away we go.

This quick, light-hearted romance from a New York Times bestselling author is sure to put a smile on your face and a song in your heart!

In Love with the Nerd is now available.

CLICK HERE to get your copy so that you can keep reading this series today!

Sneak Peek

The scrawny Rottweiler's eyes connected with Charlie's through the TV screen, begging her to save him. What if nobody else called in? What if she was his last chance at finding a home? Well, shoot. She couldn't just let him die.

Charlie grabbed her cell phone, called the local news station hosting the adoptable pets segment, and signed on the dotted line. Not once did she think she might be making a mistake. Not once did she consider the fact she'd been unable to commit to a man—or even a roommate—longer than two measly months.

And now she planned to commit to a one-year-old canine coming straight out of a neglected past?

Well, adventure had certainly found her, whether she'd asked for it or not.

The rescue volunteers didn't ask her many questions before inviting her to visit the kennel and come pick him up. If they had, maybe she'd have changed her mind.

She might have seen this as a move with the potential of becoming the biggest mistake of her entire life. Worse than the time she'd left mid-semester her junior year to travel to India in search of the answer to life. Worse than the time she'd gotten so caught up in the excitement of *V for Vendetta* she'd shaved her head in homage. Even worse than the time she'd practically eloped with a guy she'd only dated three weeks, because it seemed like a good and wildly romantic idea at the time.

At least she'd talked herself out of that one.

But what good did escaping one bad decision do, if she'd just replaced it with another by committing herself to a strange dog for—what?—ten years?

Charlie took a deep breath and gripped the steering wheel until her knuckles turned white. No going back now. She may have been impulsive, but she had a heart, darn it, and she wouldn't abandon a dog no one else wanted in the first place. Definitely too late to change her mind at this point.

"Now or never," she said to the hula dancer figurine on her dashboard before grabbing her purse and slamming the car door behind her.

"Oh, you must be Charlotte Rockwell." A volunteer with a sloppy button-up shirt and a way-too-large smile greeted her the second she entered the shelter.

Charlie nodded, pretending her feet were one million pound weights gluing her to the linoleum floor below—the only way she'd be able to avoid making a break for it.

"I'm Angela. Come on and follow me to the back." Her oversized smile grew even larger as she turned and trotted toward the back of the building.

Charlie's eyes darted to the floor to check if Angela's shoes sported actual springs.

"I'm sure Ruby told you everything you need to know when she stopped by for the home check, right?"

She nodded, even though she didn't have the slightest idea who Ruby was. The woman certainly hadn't been by her house for a visit.

"Perfect! Rugby's such a sweet boy once you get to know him. I'm so glad he's finally found a good home. You must be thrilled."

Once you get to know him?

What did *that* mean?

She was *this close* to changing her mind and dashing straight out of there, but then they pushed through the large metal door to the kennel and Rugby glanced up at her with those same sad eyes that had melted her heart in the first place.

She was officially a goner.

"Hi, Rugby," Angela cooed. "Look who it is. Your new mommy's come to take you home. Who's a good boy? Yes, you are."

Charlie sank to a squatting position and stuck her index finger through the metal fencing.

Rugby stretched and raised himself into a sitting position. He sniffed her hand delicately and gave her a huge sloppy lick.

"Oh, see. You two are perfect! Best buds already," Angela squealed. She rattled off a litany of instructions, shoved a folder of paperwork into one hand, and the leash to Charlie's new 115-pound baby in the other, and together dog and woman headed home.

Will Porter stifled a laugh as he watched the petite blonde tear into the dog park at the end of her

Rottweiler's leash. Hardly three seconds passed as they sprinted from the parking lot to the first entry gate.

When the girl unhitched the second entry gate, her dog ran away at lightning speed, not even allowing her to remove his leash. Her eyes darted from side to side as if to make sure nobody had witnessed the mishap.

Luckily, Will looked away before she could catch him staring. He allowed his gaze to settle on her again as she ran after her squatting dog with a plastic baggie cupped over her hand.

Despite the circumstances, he couldn't ignore her beauty. Blond hair escaped from her ponytail and clung to her cheeks in tendrils. Her delicate lips and nose were balanced by huge brown eyes and thick lashes. She almost reminded him of....

He snapped his attention away. Couldn't be thinking like that. Not today. He needed a distraction, and fast.

"Tuck!"

Will's golden retriever jogged over and nuzzled his thigh.

"Good boy." As he scratched the dog's head, he sensed her eyes on him, but he refused to look—

refused to give her any reason to come over and start a conversation. When had he become such a bitter old man?

He was hardly thirty—way too young to write off the opposite sex altogether. He should still be in his party phase, living it up and flirting with any pretty girl who happened to look his way. But, no, he wasn't like that—even though he often wished he were. Would have saved him the heartache of....

He grabbed the ball Tuck had dropped at his feet and hurled it toward the horizon as hard as he could. The dog raced after it in a blur of golden fur and pounding feet.

Too late, he noticed the massive black blur moving in on the ball from the opposite side of the park.

"Rugby, no!" the blonde girl screamed, but her reprimand fell on deaf ears.

The two dogs reached the ball at the exact same time. The Rottweiler bared his teeth, a low growl emanating from his throat, but Tuck wouldn't back down. The poor dog didn't even realize what was about to happen. Why would he? He'd never run into such an aggressive, undertrained beast before.

Tuck barked an invitation for the other dog to

play, and Will took off running to save his poor, over-trusting pet from the inevitable fight.

The hairs on the back of the Rottweiler's back bristled. His growl grew louder, and he lunged.

"Rugby, no!" The girl raced toward the dogs.

Tuck whimpered and ran back to Will, but the other dog slinked after him with a predatory gait.

"Hey, lady. How about controlling your dog?" he spat.

The blonde grabbed the end of the leash that was still attached to her dog and pulled him back. "I'm so sorry. I...." A sudden onslaught of tears overwhelmed her words.

Great.

Now Will felt like a bigger monster than her stupid dog.

"Hey, it's okay. Tuck's just fine. No harm done." He patted the dog's head and turned toward the other side of the park, but before he could gain much distance, she spoke again.

"Really, I'm sorry. I've only had Rugby for a few days, and I don't have a clue what I'm doing. I thought if I brought him here, I'd see how more experienced people act with their dogs. Maybe learn a thing two. I don't know." She sniffed back a tear and stared up at him with large, brown eyes—eyes far too familiar for his liking.

Why did she get such a difficult breed if she knows nothing about taking care of a dog? Will couldn't help but wonder. Still, he felt like he should offer something helpful before parting ways.

"Good luck with your training. Try watching *The Dog Whisperer* maybe."

His hold on her eyes broke when Rugby stood on his hind legs to lick the tears from his owner's face.

She chuckled and gently pushed the Rottweiler back on all fours, then wiped the slobber from her cheeks with the backs of her hands. Turning serious again, she said, "Thanks, I will, but... I just don't know what to do. I'm his last chance. The shelter had him for weeks. He even appeared on the adoptable pet segment of the news three separate times. Nobody wanted him except me. If I can't make it work, I'm practically signing his death warrant."

Will frowned. What could he say to that?

"Hey, your dog is really well-behaved. Maybe you can help us?"

Uh-oh. He didn't want to spend time with a girl who reminded him way too much of the woman who'd turned him off love altogether, but at the same time, he couldn't refuse if it meant saving the dog's life.

"I—I'll pay. I'll pay whatever it takes. Only, please help us." She tucked a strand of hair behind her ear and offered a weak smile.

"Okay, sure," he gave in. "And don't worry, you don't have to pay me anything." He didn't return her smile. He couldn't let her think he was doing this for any other reason than to save the dog.

"Oh, thank you. Thank you so much!" She wrapped her arms around him in a tight hug. "You have no idea how much you're helping me. Thank you, thank you, thank you."

Warmth spread through Will's body. He took a deep breath and let his arms go slack. She's just a girl, he reminded himself. Just a girl.

"I'm Charlotte by the way. Friends call me Charlie." She released him from the hug and tucked a strand of hair behind her other ear.

"Will." He drew a business card from his wallet. "Call me, and we'll set something up."

As soon as she accepted the card, he retreated to the other side of the park and tried not to think about how her touch had stirred something deep within him.

A girl. Just a girl.

In Love with the Nerd is now available.

CLICK HERE to get your copy so that you can keep reading this series today!

Also by Melissa Storm

ALASKAN HEARTS

Get ready to fall in love with a special pack of working and retired sled dogs, each of whom change their new owners' lives for the better, and a sprawling ranch located just outside Anchorage helps its patients regain their lives, love, and futures.

The Loneliest Cottage

The Brightest Light

The Truest Home

The Darkest Hour

The Sweetest Memory

The Strongest Love

The Happiest Place

TEXAS HEARTS

Sweet and wholesome small town love stories with

the community church at their center make for the perfect feel-good reads!

A Summer in Sweet Grove

A Supper in Sweet Grove

A Sunday in Sweet Grove

A Wedding in Sweet Grove

Someone in Sweet Grove

CHARLESTON HEARTS

A very special litter of Chihuahua puppies born on Christmas day is adopted by the local church and immediately set to work as tiny therapy dogs.

A New Life

A Fresh Start

A Surprise Visit

THE SUNDAY POTLUCK CLUB

This group of friends met in the cancer ward of the

local hospital. They've been there for each other through the hard times. Now it's time to heal...

Home Sweet Home

The Sunday Potluck Club

Wednesday Walks and Wags

Manic Monday, Inc.

THE ALASKA SUNRISE ROMANCES

Brothers, sisters, cousins, and friends—are all about to learn that love has a way of finding you when you least expect it.

In Love with the Veterinarian

In Love with the Ski Instructor

In Love with the Slacker

In Love with the Nerd

In Love with the Doctor

In Love with the Football Player

In Love with the Rodeo Rider

In Love with the Pastor

In Love with the Paramedic

SWEET STAND-ALONES

Whether climbing ladders in the corporate world or taking care of things at home, every woman has a story to tell.

About the Author

Melissa Storm loves a good cry. She believes, that whether happy or sad, tears have a way of cleansing the soul. Perhaps that's why her books have been known to make readers grab the nearest box of tissues and clutch it tight while visiting her fictional worlds. Hey, happily ever afters mean that much more when they're hard won, right?

As a *New York Times* and multiple *USA Today* bestselling author, Melissa is always juggling at least half a dozen new story ideas at any given time. She is married to fellow author Falcon Storm, mom to a precocious human princess, and keeper to an entire domestic zoo full of very spoiled cats and canines. Melissa is the owner of Novel Publicity and also writes under the name of Molly Fitz.

Find Melissa on Facebook @MeetTheStorms or sign up for her newsletter and receive an exclusive free story, *Angels in Our Lives*, along with new release alerts, themed giveaways, and uplifting messages from Melissa at **melstorm.com/gift**

Printed in Great Britain
by Amazon